HIDE & SEEK

JEROME SILBERT

HIDE & SEEK

by

Jerome G. Silbert

ISBN: 979-8-9882083-3-4

Library of Congress Control Number: T X u 2 - 3 8 8 - 2 8 2

Table of Contents

Chapter One 9

Chapter Two 11

Chapter Three 14

Chapter Four 17

Chapter Five 19

Chapter Six.. 25

Chapter Seven 29

Chapter Eight... 32

Chapter Nine 35

Chapter Ten 39

Chapter Eleven 42

Chapter Twelve 45

Chapter Thirteen... 48

Chapter Fourteen 53

Chapter Fifteen 58

Chapter Sixteen 63

Chapter Seventeen 67

Chapter Eighteen... 72

Chapter Nineteen 76

Chapter Twenty 80

Chapter Twenty-One 84

Chapter Twenty-Two 87

Chapter Twenty-Three 93

Chapter Twenty-Four 97

Chapter Twenty-Five 99

Chapter Twenty-Six 104

Chapter Twenty-Seven 108

Chapter Twenty-Eight 114

Chapter Twenty-Nine 118

Chapter Thirty 121

Chapter Thirty-One 124

Chapter Thirty-Two 129

Chapter Thirty-Three 133

Chapter Thirty-Four 138

Chapter Thirty-Five 141

Chapter Thirty-Six 145

Chapter Thirty-Seven 149

Chapter Forty 163

Chapter Forty-One 167

Chapter Forty-Two 170

Chapter Forty-Three 174

Chapter Forty-Four 178

Chapter Forty-Five 182

Chapter Forty-Six 185

Chapter Forty-Seven 189

Chapter Forty-Eight 195

Chapter Forty-Nine 200

Chapter Fifty-One 206

Chapter Fifty-Two 210

Chapter Fifty-Three 213

Chapter Fifty-Four 216

Chapter Fifty-Five 220

Chapter Fifty-Six 223

Chapter Fifty-Seven 230

Chapter One

The adage that nothing good happens after two a.m. is an incomplete warning. What happens after two begins hours before. It's conceived in the hours when day fights the coming night. Giving in, as darkness snuffs out the last of the sun's rays. That's when the original plan is born. But sometime between then and two there is a change. All reasonable, because a person is defined as reasonable. The hour drew near dawn when the sound came. Distant at first, barely noticeable, and then louder, shriller, the unmistakable wail of a siren.

* * *

"You've got to go now," Nicole said, pulling the blanket over her.

"Now? Why? It's still dark out. Isn't it?"

Her eyes, only minutes, or was it seconds before, had burned with lust but now filled with a different hue…contempt…anger?

"James, don't make me…"

"Okay, I get it. It was Jimmy earlier, but I understand. The music has stopped, and you played your song." He swung his legs off the bed and reached for his underwear.

He dressed, missing a buttonhole on his shirt. He picked his jacket from the floor. "For the record," he said, holding the door, "it was nice." She hadn't gotten out of bed but sat up. The blanket slid from her shoulders. It wouldn't be the first time she changed her mind. He lingered a second or two.

"Leave. I'll call you later."

There was no equivocation in her voice. Did she want her nakedness sealed in his brain to lure him again? *What the hell?* It worked. He unlocked the front door and didn't close it quietly. He took the elevator. The slowness of it made the images of Nicole last longer. His car was parked three blocks away. That was one of her rules. He got in, then drove past her place. A light shone from her apartment. He couldn't imagine why. By the time he was several streets away he picked up the sharp sound that pierced the quiet of the night.

Chapter Two

"Look what the cat dragged in," Lori said as Jim stepped through the front entrance. "Hell of an emergency."

She stood by the bedroom door dressed in her flannel pajamas. Pins and rollers stuck through her dark brown hair.

"Tell me honestly, how you sleep with all…?" He pointed to her head.

"If you were around more, you'd know I sleep fine." With her hand on her hip, she said, "I don't do this every night." She watched as he took off his coat. A tight smile crossed her lips as she locked onto his shirt. "About that emergency… did it require you taking off your…. uhm, clothes?"

"What? Are you crazy?" He looked down and realized his mistake. "I must have been walking around like this all night. Damn. Why didn't you tell me?"

She stepped towards him, "Hmm, your boss…that bitch…needed something in a hurry. What Nicole wants, Nicole gets."

He took a step back. "Jesus, Lor, that's not fair. You didn't like her from the beginning. You said when you first met her that she slept her way to the position."

She smiled. "Yes, I did, and I was right. Wasn't I? It should have been you, but all you have is a cock…I think."

"Shut up. It's late. I'm going to bed."

"Didn't you already do that? Bed, that is."

He glared at her while he finished unbuttoning his shirt. "You're jealous, that's all. I got a raise, and you didn't. Too bad. Maybe if you did something with that hair of yours and dressed more like a woman than a goddamn Victorian prude, you'd be noticed not just socially but professionally."

She returned the glare before stalking off to the bedroom. She turned before slamming the door. "You're a slut. Don't know why I bother to stay. There's nothing here anymore."

"I'm glad I'm sleeping in the living room. The thought of sharing a bed with you…" He didn't finish the sentence, before her door banged shut. "Bitch." She probably didn't hear him, but he felt better saying it. He took one more look toward their bedroom, then threw several of the ornamental pillows off the couch and sat. He would have been wiser to dwell on the hurt his girlfriend of five years felt, but not tonight. Instead, he grabbed one of the plusher head rests she adamantly instructed him never to lie on and did just that. The ugly scene just played was replaced in memory by Nicole's frenzied phone call instructing him to drop whatever he was doing and help in her emergency. He understood exactly what she meant.

He was smooth, in his mind at least, in creating the appropriate tone leaving their dinner outing with another couple he tolerated but Lori adored. As he held the phone to his ear and heard Nicole's velvety voice extolling all the delicious things they would do, he kept his face serious answering with many, "I understand." He even argued and looked at the ceiling with disgust. The call lasted a few minutes. When he hung up, he cleared his throat. "That was my boss, the bitch. I can't believe…"

Tom, the husband of Lori's good friend, took a gulp of his $18 bourbon, and after swallowing said, "Can't believe she'd make you come in on a Friday night. Jesus, that's shitty."

"Bosses can do that," he said. "They think they're gods. You know how that goes. It's the price paid for a better future."

Lori placed her hand over Jim's. "Not the first time, Tom. She has no boundaries. This happens so frequently. Doesn't matter the time of day or night. It's gotten to the point I asked Jim to look for another job. Hell, employees have rights, too."

Jim nodded. "Look, I'm sick of this too, but if I leave, they'd probably fire you. Besides, we both make a good living. We both know the potential is great. Plus, the job comes with lots of benefits." *I almost laughed my ass off after saying that.*

Chapter Three

ori put her ear to her closed door and listened. Hearing nothing more than Jim tossing the pillows he hated, she went to a disguised cabinet drawer of her dresser and retrieved a bottle of scotch along with a glass. Then, she retreated to the bathroom. She poured a drink and caught her reflection in the mirror. The image staring back wasn't sexy. Then again, she and Jim had known each other for seven years, five of them sharing a household. Not every night was a party. What couple has that kind of stamina or desire? Besides, truth be told, he wasn't that good. Not only now but even when they began to date.

She took a large mouthful of the liquor that made her cough. The stuff wasn't top shelf, but it would do. What the hell happened? It all changed when that bitch, Nicole, became Jim's supervisor. How long had it been? She had the month and day locked in her memory… September 12th, another Friday night. She and Jim had a family engagement that suddenly changed. He told her there was a crisis and Nicole ordered him to return to the office. She should have known, but… she took another gulp of the scotch. That was some three months ago. What did Nicole see in him?

His lovemaking was like a numbers painting. First, the bra, which 9 out of 10 times he twisted and fumbled. He'd fail even after she'd take several deep breaths to assist. It hurt and didn't pay to wait. She'd take the matter into her own hands and voilà, free her breasts. He'd attack them as if they were a video game, except there were no beeps. After he'd lose interest, or whatever, he'd plant several kisses running down her body, then some touches, probably to determine if she was ready and… Only on rare occasions did they really get into it. And when that happened, it was, she admitted, magical. The boy had potential.

She turned the faucet on to wash her face. The bloom wasn't off the rose. Her skin was wrinkle-free and taut on her high cheek bones. She took the rollers and pins out of her hair and shook it free. *Not bad, not bad at all.* Men would be attracted if she wanted. Hell, it wouldn't take much.

She straightened and sat on her makeup chair. She didn't want that. Jim took her from that world of dating, pretending, wondering. He didn't rescue her. It seemed they were on the same page, wanting the same things, tired of the single life. She thought they were happy. They weren't rich, but comfortable and didn't want for much. They griped about their work, sometimes each other, but everyone did.

She refilled her glass. She tried to picture Nicole and Jim in bed. Had his technique improved? Why Nicole?

She finished most of the bottle and was buzzed. She got up from her chair and stumbled toward the bedroom. Her thoughts went from Jim fucking the bitch to figuring out the number of drinks she'd had, including dinner. She felt her way around her bed before she plopped on it. "Jesus, I'm drunk," was the last thing she said.

* * *

Jim got as comfortable as he could on the couch. He knew its nooks and crannies. It wasn't the first time he'd spent the night on it. It would take a while, but eventually sleep would come. He moved the pillow around, searching for the cold spot. Then, after listening for any other sounds from Lori's bedroom, switched to something more pleasant… Nicole. She appeared at a time he must have been looking but didn't know it. The humdrum of the life he knew morphed into an intensity never imagined. The sex was the icing. It was what led up to it that made the air rarefied and put that extra bounce in his step. Her voice, the way she didn't just move, but glided as if God gave her the ability of flight. She was the very definition of grace and beauty. Why should he feel guilty about getting a gift this rare? He deserved it. The thought gratified him, even brought a smile as to his good fortune. A small sigh escaped. He drifted toward sleep picturing Nicole's naked body lying in bed.

Chapter Four

Rain, sheets of rain, hit the top of the window air conditioner hand stirred Lori's consciousness. Each drop sounded like a very near explosion. She lifted one eyelid, then the other. Her mouth felt like she'd swallowed balls of cotton. Reality tiptoed slowly. She never made it under the covers. The ceiling above her seemed curved, but that was impossible. She played with that thought, anyway. Sistine Chapel? Michelangelo? "Do it over. I don't like all those things flying above me," she said to the very dead artist. She shut her eyes for a second or two. When she opened them again, the Chapel and the master painter were no longer there. Her stomach growled and her head weighed an enormous amount. *I'll never drink again,* she told herself, but knew despite the haze and dizziness, it was a promise never to be kept.

"Jim, you there?" Then remembered he was on the couch, not next to her. While she gathered the strength to make it to the bathroom, last night's events seeped through the fog. "Jesus." Nausea raced from her stomach to her throat and with surprising speed she made it to the toilet in time. She flushed, then hung onto the bowl for what seemed a while, the coldness of the porcelain unexpected comfort.

The rain was now a steady beat. Her bedroom still dark as well as the bathroom. A perfect reflection of her mood. She inched her way up, gripping the toilet, then the sink for balance. She'd go back to bed. Hell, it was Saturday, wasn't it? She had to think. Yes, last night was… oh yeah. She stumbled her way, taken aback that out of nowhere she began to cry. She muffled her tears in her pillow. She didn't want to give Jim the satisfaction of her hurt. She'd suffer alone.

Get a grip, she told herself as she regained control. She dried her face with the shams and sat up. *It couldn't still be night?* She turned to the bedside table, working hard to read the numerals on the clock radio. *Fuck, it's early morning…just after seven…too early to do anything but sleep.* She had another thought. It concerned Jim, but it flew away when… someone pounded on a door.

"Jim? What's going on?" She slid her feet off the bed and went to her bedroom door. She heard muffled voices, then a crash. Almost simultaneously she swung her door open. A number of persons—was it 3 or 4—with guns in their hands rushed through the house.

"Freeze. Get on the floor," someone shouted. "Police."

She fell. "What? Who are you?" Her head was raised at the approaching officers.

"Shut up. What's your name?" Jones was written on his nametag.

"Lori…Lori Knight. What's… what's going on?"

"You live here?"

"Yes. Please tell—"

"You have ID?"

"Yeah, but I'm in my pajamas. Can I sit?"

He motioned with the flick of his weapon. "Search her," he ordered a female officer named O'Brien.

Lori was ordered to stand, and O'Brien patted her down.

"She's clear. Have a seat on the couch."

"Who are you?" Lori heard another cop ask Jim, who was sitting.

Lori was led, then pushed to a place at the far end. She saw Jim's face. It was pale, almost white, and his eyes were wide. A drop of sweat dripped from his hairline and his right hand trembled slightly.

"Do either of you know a Nicole McMaster?"

"We work at the same place," Lori said.

"Yeah?" The one named Jones came closer. "That's no longer the case."

"Whatcha mean?" Jim started to rise.

"Get your ass back on that couch. She's dead."

Chapter Five

ori stared blankly at the wall. "I don't...sorry... I'm confused. Why am I at the police station? Where's Jim?"

"You have a right to remain silent. You have the right to have an attorney present," Detective Young read off her Admonition of Rights card.

"What?"

Young sighed. "Ma'am, I'm reading you your rights. You understand what I'm saying?"

Lori shook her head. "No... I really don't. What does this have to do with me? Do I need a lawyer? Am I under arrest?"

Young ignored the inquiries and continued reading from her card. "Anything you say can and will be used against you. You can stop at any time. You got that?" She didn't wait for an answer and slid a piece of paper to Lori. "Sign this."

Lori saw the detective's mouth move, but everything said was like background music. The voice had no articulation. Lori told herself to concentrate. She knew the detective was saying something. She stared at the officer and noticed the gun on the detective's belt, but her comprehension abilities continued to fail.

Too much scotch, too much...fear, anger, embarrassment. Her stomach growled loudly. Lori felt her face redden. She'd never been in a police station in her life, much less handcuffed and whisked away. The neighbors probably saw. Hell, her bosses will know, and what of her family? She, Lori Knight, graduated with honors from Michigan. The pride of her mom and dad, now sitting in a police station unable to understand a single word spoken.

"Ms. Knight, did you hear what I said?" Young pointed to the paper. "Read it and sign. It's an acknowledgement you've been advised of your rights."

Lori glanced from the detective to the sheet in front of her. "Rights? What rights? Am I under arrest?"

"I'll repeat it once again. You do speak and understand English?"

"English… yes… I…I majored in it."

"Great." Young said it with an air of disgust. "Then stop playing games and make it easy on yourself."

Lori squinted. The detective had her hair in a bob and wore a beige shirt with a "Chicago Police" emblem.

Was that a command? A suggestion? The way out? "Okay… I don't mean to give you a hard time. I'm… well… confused about the whole situation. One minute I'm in bed, the other you folks bust into my house pointing guns. I'm trying to process all this."

Young didn't respond. She pointed to the paper and told her to sign.

Lori picked up the pen and wrote her name.

"Okay, we can start. Detective Brandt will be joining us. Everything done and said in this room is being recorded. That's done for your protection as well as ours. Understand?"

Lori searched the room for the cameras but didn't see them. "Yeah, I guess." She folded her hands and took in a deep breath.

On cue the door opened, and Detective Brandt stepped in. He appeared to be in his late 30s, early 40s. His hair was chestnut brown, and the sides were over his ears. He had a trim beard and very blue eyes. He introduced himself and pulled out the chair across from Lori. He slapped a large see-through baggie on the table. Jewelry glistened through the plastic. He opened the bag and took one of the pieces out.

"Do you recognize this?"

Lori stared at it as if it was a snake about to bite. "It's… it's a ring… sapphire I guess."

"Yours?"

She shook her head.

"How about this?" Brandt took a bracelet from the envelope.

"No. What is this? I don't have jewelry like that. Those look like diamonds. Jesus, expensive. Not my taste."

"Ever see them before?"

"What? I… what are you really asking?"

Brandt gave Young a side look. "We found these in your car."

The remnants of last night's scotch threatened to come back up. She quickly covered her mouth and swallowed hard. Her shoulders shook while she gasped for breath. "No….no…. my car… no."

Brandt went into another envelope. "Here's the picture. That's your car, isn't it? That's your glove compartment. That's the Secretary of State's license sticker card with your name."

Lori looked at the picture in a trance. A quirky thought popped into her head. If she stared at the photo intensely enough, maybe she'd have Superman's powers and the rays from her eyes would burn the damn thing.

"Ms. Knight, are you there?" Detective Young's voice brought her back.

"Listen, I… I don't know where you got these things. I never saw them before and I'm pretty sure Jim hasn't either. I want to go home. I want a lawyer."

* * *

Jim sat in another interview room at the police station with his hands folded. The temperature fluctuated from warm to chilly.

He took in his surroundings. There were no clocks or pictures on the walls. The table was nondescript with four plastic chairs around it. The walls were painted a yellowish beige. The top of the door had some sort of glass, and the rest was metal.

Time passed slowly. It must be at least sometime in the afternoon. He got tired of staring at the walls or ceiling. Instead, he began to run scenarios through his mind as to what will happen. Then he heard a click and the metal door opened and two officers came in.

"I'm Detective Brandt and this is Detective Young," Brandt said. "You've been advised of your rights?"

Jim nodded. "Listen, I…eh… want to… no bullshit. I had an affair with Nicole…Ms. McMaster. You probably know I was at her place this morning." He leaned forward. "I want to make this clear. When I left, she was very much alive."

Brandt held up his hand to stop any more conversation. "I want to make sure you know that everything you say is being taken down and could be used against you."

"I got it. I've committed no crime. Affairs aren't against the law."

Brandt gave Young a quick glance. "You're right about that. When did the affair start?"

Jim leaned back. "I'd say about five or six months ago."

"Did your wife know?"

"My…? Lori? She's not my wife. We've lived together for, hmm, five or six years. Did she know? Not right away, but probably figured it out."

"When do you think she caught on?"

"Certainly, before yesterday. I don't know… a few months ago."

"What made you think that?"

Jim cleared his throat. "I don't know if either of you have been in relationships, but you know. It's in their eyes. The way they respond. The snide remarks. There's a change in attitude."

Brandt switched subjects. "You and Lori work at the same place?"

"Yeah, but different departments. She edits. I research. You probably already know Nicole was my boss. She and I vied for the same position, but she got it. She was much better looking."

Detective Young grimaced, then placed an envelope on the table. "What time did you get to Ms. McMaster's apartment?"

Jim shifted his weight and glanced around the room. "Hard to say, but it was… Lori and I were out to dinner with another couple. Nicole called and I made excuses and left. It was near midnight. I stopped on the way and bought a bottle of champagne. Nicole gets a kick out of that. By the time I showed, it was probably after one, maybe one-thirty."

"What time did you leave her place?"

"Geez, after three…not sure."

"Did you go straight home?"

Jim's palms became sweaty, and he dried them on his pants. "Look, I didn't keep a time clock." Young's stare never left him. "Okay, no, I didn't. I stopped at a bar."

"At three-thirty in the morning?"

He shrugged.

"What's the name?"

He looked from one detective to another. "Jesus, Orphans on Lincoln. I think."

"How long did you stay?"

Jim wiped his face with his hand. "Not sure. Had one drink, then left."

"Was Lori home when you returned?"

"Oh yeah. She wasn't happy with me. That's how I landed on the couch."

Young undid the flap of the envelope and withdrew a photo. "Is this your car?"

Jim moved forward and looked. "Yep. Looks like my Beemer. Has my plates."

"Does Lori drive it?"

"No, seldom. She has her car, and I have mine."

"Was Nicole in your car?"

"No. I don't think she ever was in my Beemer."

Brandt reached down for another envelope. He opened it and took out a leopard-spotted thong. "You recognize this?"

Jim's jaw dropped. "I…eh… yeah. Where did…"

"Was this Nicole's?"

Jim blinked. His memory took him to the early morning. Nicole greeted him at the door wearing that or one that was identical and one of his shirts, unbuttoned. There was little or no conversation. She took the champagne, laughed, and said, "Later". It was all about fucking.

"Jim, are you here?"

He looked down at the table. "Yeah, yes. Nicole was wearing that this morning."

"Did you take it?"

"Of course not. Why?"

"We found it in your car behind the driver's side."

"What the hell?"

Chapter Six

Lori was told she could leave. Just like that, she was freed. Detective Brandt warned her not to take any trips to faraway places. Like where or why would she? The dick asked her if she had a way to get home. She shrugged… "Jim?"

"He'll be detained a while longer. I'll call a cab for you."

Brandt led her through a door that opened into the front of the station. To her left was a large semi-circular counter behind which several uniformed cops directed various complainants and defendants.

She couldn't get out of the station fast enough. She could smell her sweat and didn't have to lift her arm. When she put her jacket sleeve to her face, an odor of mustiness. She rubbed her wrists and saw the faded outline of handcuffs. She decided to wait outside and was struck that the day was gone. She pulled her phone from her purse and couldn't believe the time. *Holy crap, talk about a waste.*

The cabbie pulled up. Lori climbed into the back seat of his multicolored taxi. The driver was young, skinny, and had a short dirty-blond ponytail. He wore large glasses. After repeating her address, she sat back. Of course, after the day she had, she winds up with a hippy dippy driver. Did he even shave?

No sooner had they hit the road when he began a barrage of questions. The first: "Hard day?"

Before she had a chance to respond she was struck with his second. "What's a lady like you doing at the police station at this time of night?

She wanted to dismiss it. It would be the smart thing to do, but… So simple a question what the hell was the answer? She caught bits of his follow-ups.

"Accident? Were you arrested?" She saw him look in the rear-view mirror, sizing her up. "Did you get busted for dope? Sex?

Hell, I've driven several ho's, I mean prostitutes. Turns out they were really nice. Not like the movies. Just people. Some were lookers if you know what I mean."

She caught his gaze in the mirror. She wanted to ask where she fit but thought better. "It's none of the above," she broke her silence.

That shut him up for a few minutes, but he continued to check the mirror more than necessary. What he wanted was becoming too obvious. She chuckled and was somewhat amazed that a man, despite her looking like an unmade bed, still wanted to fuck. Jesus.

* * *

Brandt watched his computer screen from inside his cubbyhole of an office as Lori got into the cab. The outside camera relayed the picture. He then joined Young at the coffee machine in the center of an open area on the second floor. "What do you think?"

"About Jimbo? He's got an answer for everything."

Brandt filled his cup. "Let him sit a few more minutes. "What about his girlfriend?"

"Which? The dead one or the one who walked."

Brandt smiled. "Very good. I mean Lori. You think she played a part?"

Young shrugged. "Too early to tell. I'd like the autopsy. How long before we get it?"

Brandt took a sip. "Man, this is terrible stuff. The only thing that makes this shit coffee is its color." He dumped several spoonfuls of sugar into the cup and sampled. "Better, but…"

"Keep doing that, Brandt, and you'll be a diabetic in no time."

He grunted, then slurped another sip. "You think this stuff is good?"

She shrugged. "I'm a diet cola person, myself. Never touch what you're drinking."

"That's what gets you started in the morning…diet crap?"

"One person's crap is another's gold," she said, smiling.

Brandt eyed her. Youth still graced her face. He believed there was a very feminine figure hidden underneath the drab pants and CPD polo shirt. But to go down that road was job-dangerous. Much easier to keep the relationship collegiate and professional.

They had worked three cases together and he knew she took no bullshit. By the book, yes, but sometimes her book had missing pages. "What do we have so far?"

"Suspicion, not much more." Young was quick with her answer. "We still don't know cause of death. There's no knife wound or gunshot. Hell, maybe her heart gave out after Jim gave her a ride of a lifetime. Stranger things have happened."

Brandt held his reinforced paper cup in front of him. "Makes sense, but what's Nicole's jewelry doing in Lori's car? Or Nicole's thong in his. There's more to it. Besides, Jim gives off bad vibes. As for Lori, I agree, too early to tell. Shall we have another go at Jim?"

"After you."

* * *

Jim remained seated at the table. The cops asked him if he needed to use the bathroom or wanted water or coffee. When he said no, they left him in the room that he guessed he'd been for the entire day. It occurred to him that all the waiting, the dicks going in and out, was an interrogation ploy. Hell, he'd seen too many movies and TV shows. He was wise to the game. Let the "perp" soak in his own juices. Well…he drummed his fingers on the table, replaying pop standards in his head. It didn't take long before he tired or ran out of melodies. He abruptly got up and walked around the small room. Should he try the door? Part of him was willing, but then realized there were cameras watching his every move. He plopped back on his plastic chair and stared at the wall.

Several thoughts rushed him at once. Lori. Were the cops still talking to her? What did she tell them? What could she tell them? He smiled…not much. Nicole. Dead. Hard to believe. Why? Who would want to? He heard the click of the door. He glanced over.

The two dicks, Brandt and Young, stepped in. Their faces gave nothing away.

Chapter Seven

Lori thought of asking the cab driver to drop her off a few blocks from her home. She needed air and was tired of being confined. The walk would do her good. Besides, she was uncomfortable with the creepy driver knowing her address. What was she thinking? Of course, he knew where she lived. She sighed, then grabbed the door handle.

"Hey, let me off at the next block."

"I'll take you to your door."

"That's okay. I need the exercise."

His gaze shot through the mirror. The intensity sought to pierce her clothing. "You sure?"

She nodded. "Oh yeah. Here would be fine."

He stopped at the corner of Devon and Forrest Glen. "The fare is $25."

She reached into her purse, the pocket of her coat, then her jeans. Shit, the cops dragged her out this morning before she could check everything. "Ah, I…left…without…oh… Damn."

"Not even a credit card?"

She shook her head and struggled not to cry.

"Lady, the tear crap don't work. Happens too often." He turned towards her. His eyes danced with mischief. "In this business, you know, there are other ways to pay."

She stared at him in disbelief this was happening.

"I'm just say'n. You wouldn't want me to call the cops."

She met his gaze. "Take me home. You'll get your money."

"Sure, lady, but don't think I'll stay in the cab waiting. Nobody stiffs me." He laughed at his own pun.

The cabbie drove up the driveway. Lori didn't wait for the taxi to come to a complete stop. "Don't even think of following me into my house. I'll be right back." She jumped out.

"Right, lady."

She heard him open his door as she hurried to the back. She snatched the spare key from its hiding place under a planter and even though her hand shook she managed to fit the key into the lock and open the back door. She flicked on lights and spotted her wallet on the floor in the kitchen. She grabbed it and went to the front.

She had barely caught her breath when she opened the front door. The driver stood within a foot of her.

"For a moment, I thought you ditched me, and I'd have to call the cops. But here you are." He held the screen door open. "You're lucky I'm a patient guy."

"Don't take a step further. Here's your money." She thrusted a bundle of bills at him.

He grabbed her wrist. "Honey, didn't you get my drift? Do I have to spell it out for you?"

"Let go. I'm giving you the money." She stared at him.

He held onto her for a few seconds longer before he took what was in her hand. "Okay, if that's the way you want to play it. I mean, you've got a nice place here. You must be a ho in demand. But I get it, not for guys like me. No problem. Just because I'm young and don't have cool duds." He remained close to her. "I'd give you a ride better than any of the pretty boys you do."

"Get the hell out, before I call your boss and the police."

He let go of the screen as she slammed the door. She leaned against the frame panting, then listened. It seemed like forever but finally she heard the roar of an engine and squealing of tires. She counted to ten, then opened the door a smidge. The driveway was empty.

* * *

Jim didn't wait for the dicks' questioning. He was tired, hungry, and had had enough.

"Listen, there's not more to tell. I had an affair. That's not law enforcement stuff. That's between me and Lori. Nicole was alive when I left. We had sex and then she told me to leave. I did. I can't believe she's dead."

Brandt glanced at Jim, then waited for Young to tear into him. Several seconds passed before she began.

"You understand we're doing our job. A good-looking woman was found dead minutes after you left. That makes you a person of interest."

"You say you found her minutes after I left? How? Did someone call? I'm confused."

Young looked at her yellow pad. "You're right, someone called. It was Nicole."

"Nicole? What…what did she say?" Jim's hand shook.

"We'll have the tape later. From my notes of the transcript, Nicole called 911 and said, not verbatim, that she's dying. Someone…" Young stared directly at Jim. "The rest was difficult to hear. The lab was working on it. Now is your chance to talk."

A phrase from Sonny and Cher, "It Ain't You, Babe," played in Jim's head. He looked at his interrogators. "I think we're done here. I'm going to slowly get up and leave." He glanced at the hidden cameras. "Hope you got that. I'm done."

Chapter Eight

Jim watched the two dicks whisper to each other. Finally, the woman, Young, told him he could go, but remain close to town. Like a rocket, Jim jumped out of his chair. The force nearly knocked it over. He didn't want to stay in that Godforsaken interview room a minute longer. *What if the dicks change their minds?* The detectives, though, told him there was paperwork to fill out for his personal items. They pointed to where he needed to sign, and he did. Did he read the documents? Not really. He shook his head and initialed where he was told. He heard something about a cab as he dashed out and hurried down the stairs to the main lobby. He caught his breath, then bummed a cigarette from a man whose arms were layered with tattoos. The man told Jim he had been hanging around the station for a while. "My woman supposed to get out any time now," he said. Then he raised his eyebrows. "Those fucks, you never know. Been here over an hour, waiting."

Jim thanked him for the smoke and went outside. One of the detectives, he thought it was Brandt, said he'd call a cab. Jim would have done it himself but Young confiscated his cell phone...*the bitch.*

He took a deep breath. He too was startled; the time was well into the night. He had spent the whole fuck'n day cooped up, interrogated, treated like a common criminal...*damn.*

He asked for a light from a woman whom he stopped coming out of the station. She wasn't bad looking in her tight jeans and opened jacket, but it was the wrong time for that sort of thing. He chatted her up, anyway. He intuitively understood it wasn't what was said but how. His patter was easy and unthreatening. He made little jokes, feigned interest, and before he knew it, she offered to take him for a drink. *What the hell? Où menè le coeur. Where the heart leads.* Nicole used that saying many times. And Lori? It took him less than a minute to rationalize. If she had been released, then she was at home. Without a phone he couldn't call her, and she couldn't reach him. If she wasn't, he couldn't do anything anyway. Detective Young did him a favor keeping his goddamn cell. He chuckled as he settled himself into the passenger side of his new friend's car. Things work out. They almost always do.

He turned to her. "So where are we going?" then took a long drag on the cigarette.

"Where dreams are made," she answered.

* * *

Brandt looked at his computer feed from the outside camera. "Hey, Young, you ain't goin' to believe this. Get your ass over here."

"Come on, Brandt, it's time to get the hell out of this place. What are you looking at?" She came over to his desk and watched. "I don't fuck'n believe it. That sonofabitch got into the car with... Jesus."

They exchanged glances.

"Did those two know each other?" Young asked.

"Hells bells, I don't have a clue."

It was too dark for the camera to read the license plate. In a blink of an eye the vehicle drove off.

"Did you get the make or year of the car?" Young asked.

Brandt had a pen in his hand and scribbled 'dark, sedan'. "No, it happened too quick."

"Ever see that broad around here?"

Brandt shook his head. "That blonde?" The camera hid her face in the shadows. "I would have remembered." He looked away from his computer. "Oh well, all we know is the figure looked female."

Young raised her eyebrows. A small grin played at the corners of her mouth. "I'm sure she would have stuck in your mind."

* * *

Lori turned on all the lights in the house. The incident with the ponytailed asshole cab driver left her as shaken as the police interrogation…even more. She knew she had nothing to do with Nicole's death, but… to be almost sexually assaulted or devoured by… She couldn't believe it happened. She wasn't blind, such things occur, but not to her in a million years.

She glanced at the clock in the kitchen. *Where the hell is Jim? Could it possibly be…? Oh God, that isn't Jim's character, no, never.* A philanderer, yeah guilty, but a murderer? She shook her head at the thought. It didn't make sense. Why would he kill her? Apparently having a live-in-girlfriend didn't stop him from an affair. Nor did that bother Nicole. She, Lori, was the outsider and had no say in the matter.

She grabbed one of the kitchen chairs and sank into it. All of this was too much. She needed a drink. She went to the bar area of the step-down living room, poured herself one, and took a gulp. So much for staying on the wagon. She took her drink and the bottle and settled onto the couch. The same one where Jim slept the last night. She took another sip and refilled it. *Where the fuck is Jim? Should I call the station?* Her grip tightened around the glass. Too much was happening. Too much… She sat back and felt something sharp underneath her. "Damn it." She jumped spilling some of the liquor. A key ring with three keys straddled the cushions. She picked them up to examine. They weren't the house keys or their office ones. Nicole's? *Jesus, the son of a bitch had her keys.* She let them slip from her hand in disgust. She eyed the bottle that she had placed on the coffee table. She swept her hair from her face, fighting back tears. She wasn't going to get drunk…not this time. She needed to shower. She needed to get the day's stench with all its misery to disappear.

Chapter Nine

Brandt glanced at the blackened screen while he watched Young gather her things.

"I'd say we put in a good day's work. The captain shouldn't give us shit for a while."

"Yeah, right," Young had changed into a pair of blue jeans and a black top. She had her coat in one hand and a file in the other.

"What are you doing with that?" Brandt pointed to the folder.

"This?" She held up her arm. "Review my notes. Nothing big. The autopsy better be here tomorrow."

"Right." He drummed his hand on the desk. "Yeah, it's time to go. Let me know if you find something in there that we missed."

"Sure." She paused as if she was thinking or wanted to say something, but the moment passed. "See ya tomorrow."

Brandt gave a half wave and turned back to the computer. He waited for the outside camera to pickup his partner's exit. He saw her walk towards her car until she was out of view.

"That's it," he sighed, "another day in the Garden of Eden." He got up and walked to the rear of the detective section for his coat. The second floor was quiet. He glanced at the clock on the wall... 2:00 a.m. From his years of experience, he knew what this hour of the night meant. When the bars closed, mayhem began.

He walked by the captain's office and plunked a time sheet on the desk. The skinflint will be pissed when he reads he and Young spent two hours overtime, but the case was complicated and it was "Breaking News," whatever the hell that meant.

Nicole McMaster, the deceased, was a prominent up and coming star in the business world. Why she'd jeopardize her career having an affair with Jim O'Dell, the person of interest, whom they'd just released, was a head scratcher. Of course, the number one question was how...then why?

Brandt stepped outside. The cold made him shiver as he got into his car. He put the key into the ignition and his six-year-old Ford Fusion sprang to life despite the weather. He patted the steering wheel in acknowledgement. He sat, deciding where he wanted to go. Home, of course was an option, but there wasn't much to greet him except a beer from the fridge and sleep. Or, there was Carla. That brought a smile. He sighed, then put the car in drive. He was sure she was up at this hour. He could call, but that took the fun away from arriving unexpectedly. She'd answer the door with a sheepish grin on her face. "What the hell are you doing here at this hour," she'd say. Although she knew very well why he was there.

On the way, just for the hell of it, he could stop at Nicole's place. It would only take a few minutes. He'd talk with the beat guys still protecting the scene. Maybe they saw or heard something. He was well aware in many cases small things, things not in the right place, or omitted, unlocked the puzzle.

The streets flew by as traffic was light. It was one of the reasons he liked working this shift. The other was the brass were rarely there. They had better things to do than sit in their offices. They'd make the rounds, show the flag, then tell the sergeant they were available on the mobile. Where they went, who they saw, if they were good at what they did, one never knew, until they fucked up and then it was all over the news.

He checked the time.... 2:30. His thoughts momentarily drifted to Carla. He pictured her getting ready for bed. Well, he'd be there soon.

* * *

Her name outside her work in the police department was Charlie Young. Christened Charlene but for as long as she remembered everyone called her Charlie. She liked it and one day would legally change it. She enjoyed the surprise on peoples' faces when they expected a man rather than her. It was a conversation starter and, in some cases, stopper. Either way, she liked the freedom the name represented. There were the bad jokes about "Charlie's Angels," but by now she had heard them too many times to take offense.

She also took pride in her reputation as a badass dick. She was aware of the word on the street. "That's one bitch you didn't mess with." It made her smile. In the boy's club of the Department, she'd earned that reputation. She considered herself "fair" in the administration of justice. The wisdom of other seasoned cops, and Brandt in particular, was her mantra… "Do what you have to but make sure you cover your ass."

It took a little longer than the usual twenty minutes to drive to her apartment in the Lincoln Square neighborhood. There were a few stops she had to make. Errands of sorts needed to be done at weird hours working nightshift.

Her ex-live-in boyfriend was another cop who, in her view, couldn't take her ambition and rise in the department. She threw him out a few months ago. Instead of arguments and the occasional make-up sex, her apartment was quiet. A glass of wine replaced conversation.

She went to her bedroom and took off her jeans and top and replaced them with one of her old boyfriend's leftover shirts from the closet. It wasn't sentimental, only convenient, and comfortable. Her discarded clothes were left on her unmade bed. She got herself a diet cola from the kitchen, then curled on her couch in the living room. She picked up the file brought from the station and glossed over the first page of the beat cops' report. She was sure her partner Brandt had read it carefully. She looked away from the papers for a moment and wondered what Brandt was doing. Where did he go? After working with him on three cases, she knew little about what he did outside the office. He played his private life close to the vest.

Brandt gave off a laid-back exterior. If you didn't know him, his attitude could be mistaken as lazy. Jack Brandt, his first name rarely used, was anything but. Once he got the scent, he was like a terrier, he'd bite into it and not let go. A small laugh escaped her as she envisioned Brandt as a snarling dog engaged in a tug of war.

She returned to the file and turned to page two. One of the beat cops, Williams, wrote that the victim was found on her side, naked, lying on the edge of the bed. There was no indication of a forced entry. Her bedroom was in order but for a snifter on the floor within inches of her outstretched arm. She rushed through the other pages to the inventory report. Where the fuck was the glass, or for that matter, the Champagne bottle that Jim, the person of interest, claimed to have brought? She swung her legs to the floor. She had a half a mind to drive to the scene or call Brandt, then caught herself. It wasn't a good idea, particularly for her, to act in haste. Beat cops often wrote supplementals. She sat back. No point making a rushed judgement. She'd wait.

Chapter Ten

Steam covered the mirror as Lori stepped out of the shower. The heat and pounding of the water eased some of her tension. The day's grime swirled down the bathtub drain. She reached for her fluffy white bath towel and wrapped it around her. She then brushed her hair and its wetness reminded her of stepping out of a pool after swimming 10 to 12 laps. She had been a damn good swimmer…once.

The fog dissipated and the mirror cleared. She let the towel drop slowly from her shoulders to the floor and studied her reflection. Then in a flight of foolishness posed in what she fancied were sexy positions. She still had that come-hither look and gave herself more than a passing grade. She gathered the towel and clothes and stepped into the master bedroom. She liked the sound and majesty of that concept although in some circles that term was politically incorrect. *Screw them.* Master did not necessarily mean male, but even if it did, so what. Everything in this room had her touch, her taste. *Master my ass.* What's in a name? In the end, if played right…women controlled. They had what most males wanted…sex.

She stared at the vacant bed. It was a queen. Jim wanted a king, but she persuaded him it was big enough for intimacy as well as space. Now? Where were the sparks? A grunt escaped from her throat. Staring at the emptiness, her thoughts returned to Nicole.

She pictured Nicole in her office or when she deigned to have lunch with the commoners such as herself. Nicole knew how to manipulate. She dressed on the edge of provocativeness and had the figure for it. Her body was a tool and she employed it well. Smart, yes, but that only went so far. She wanted to advance quickly, like she was running a race against an invisible competitor. Head of the department was just a step toward bigger things. Jim was such a fool. Nicole would discard him as it had been whispered about others. Her reputation wasn't exactly hidden---if one listened to gossip and hung around the right circles. Didn't Jim know? Christ, T and A blinded him to the bigger game Nicole played.

Lori went to her bureau and pulled out a flannel nightgown. What the hell. The last thing she'd want was to make love to him. He'd have to earn that, if ever. Then again, as she puffed the pillows on her side of the bed, where the hell was he?

* * *

The woman who picked Jim up from the police department sped down Central Avenue. Traffic rules appeared to be an inconvenience to be obeyed when necessary. To calm himself, he decided to make conversation. First by introducing himself as Jim.

"Well Jim, I'm called Whirley."

"Whirley? That's your given name?"

"You can say. My man thinks I'm a whirley bird so that's what he and his boys call me."

"Excuse me. Your boyfriend, husband?"

"Don't look so surprised. You bummed that cigarette off him. The poor bastard's probably still waiting."

Jim's mouth hung open.

"Am I going too fast for you?"

"Yeah, and yeah."

"The cops earlier pinched me for traffic bullshit. They tried for hooking, but I wasn't. Honest. I can smell them a mile away. It's all part of their game."

He wasn't surprised by her almost admission. He sort of liked it.

"What do you do, Jim? If that's your real name. Usually it's Bill, or Mark, or some other made-up handle. It don't make much difference. In forty-five minutes to an hour the body parts are the same no matter what the person calls themselves. So, what is it that you do?"

"I'm...eh..."

"Spill it. I've heard it all." She took her eyes off the road. "Yeah, I make you for a suit. A corporation guy whose nose is up someone's ass."

"I wouldn't...watch the damn road. Shit."

"I got it. Don't get your tighty whities in a bunch."

"Jesus." He sucked in some air. "Where the hell are we going? And for your information I don't wear..."

"Never you mind. We'll see."

"Huh?"

"This is your lucky night, Jimbo. It's on the house."

Chapter Eleven

Brandt parked at the first empty spot he saw near the corner of Astor and Schiller and walked the half block north on Astor. He was in the heart of the area in Chicago known as the Gold Coast. The brownstones and high rises that graced the street smelled of money. This Nicole McMaster either had that kind of dough or someone was paying the freight. He was pretty sure it wasn't Jim O'Dell. He spotted the undercover car idling in front of the building.

"How you doing?" Brandt said, walking up to the cop sitting in the driver's seat. He flashed his badge at the same time.

"All right. Nothing much happening but the scenery earlier was an eyeful." The driver nudged his partner. "Ain't that right, Joe."

Joe smiled and nodded.

"Glad you boys had some entertainment," Brandt said. "Anything suspicious while you've been sitting here?"

"Nope," answered the one in the driver's seat.

"What about the neighbors?"

"Curious about the police tape and us but they went about their business. There's a twenty-year- old, female on the second floor. She goes to Northwestern. Lucky college boys. Her name, hold on, I have a picture of her ID on my phone." He scrolled through dozens. "Here it is…Neve Kahn. Her father owns the place and allows her to live there. She came home sometime after two from a party. She heard a thump but didn't think much about it. Claims she doesn't know the third-floor occupant well. Enough to say hi and bye."

"How about Nicole's lover boy, Jim?"

"'fraid I didn't ask. Sorry. Here's the number if you want to call." He looked at his watch. "I caught her when she went out tonight. Another party. Haven't seen her return. Have you, Joe?"

"Nah, unless she snuck by when I reached for that sandwich in the back."

Brandt leaned into the driver's window. "What about the ones on the first floor?"

Joe answered. "Older couple...last name of Watson. They didn't even know anything happened upstairs. They go to bed early."

"Did they know Nicole or Jim?"

"The husband, Sinclair, seemed to have been more acquainted with her. Said Nicole moved in about six months ago. He did recognize the guy, Jim. He'd see him leaving around five in the morning on the weekends mostly. Thought he lived with her or something."

"Any other men visit Nicole?"

Joe wiped his face. "Didn't ask."

Brandt straightened. "Okay, boys, keep doing what you're doing. I'm going upstairs for another look-see before turning in."

Brandt entered the front lobby. The walls were mirrored, and the flooring had a marble design. The ceiling looked like Michelangelo stopped by on his way to Rome. The security door stood open. The elevator was twenty feet from there. The quaintness of it shouted its age. The gate had black grillwork and metallic birds hanging on the leaves. He questioned whether the damn thing actually worked. It looked like it came from a century-old Parisian bordello. He'd take the stairs.

The carpet on the stairs was worn. He realized as he climbed to the first and second floor landings that there was one apartment on each level. No sounds came from within any of them.

Police tape covered the outside of Nicole's front door. He ducked under and used the key he brought. The fixture on the outside landing allowed him to find the light switch for her apartment before closing her front door.

Her front hallway had parquet flooring that led into a large living room. A couch, chairs, and table looked out toward the floor to ceiling windows that made up one wall of the room. To the right was a dining room. A large Persian rug was under twelve heavily cushioned chairs that surrounded a long, sleek, polished wood table. Through French doors was a nice size kitchen furnished with all the modern accoutrements and equipment. There wasn't a dish in the sink or dishwasher. The Wolf stove looked as shiny as the day it was installed. Brandt opened the Sub-Zero refrigerator and but for three bottles of Perrier, an apple, and a half-empty package of Kraft cheese it was empty. The freezer had several frozen Amy's super-duper Chinese good-for-you-crap. He retraced his steps and entered a long hallway at the other end of the living room. There were two bedrooms and bathrooms adjacent to it. At the end of the corridor was the master bedroom. Police tape walled off the entrance.

Before Brandt walked in, he retraced his steps and went into one of the bathrooms. Although the place, he was sure, had been dusted for prints, he needed something for his hands just in case. He flicked on the light and as he reached for a tissue, he saw an ashtray hidden by assorted electric toothbrushes and a water pick on the vanity counter. The tray was filled with ash. There remained a faint smell of a tobacco product; cigar was his first choice, but it could have been cigarettes. He took out his phone and photographed the object, then left the room and went back through the apartment. Not one ashtray in the place. He checked all the cabinet drawers in all the other bedrooms and bathrooms. Then re-examined the living room and kitchen cabinets but didn't find any cigarettes, cigars, blunts, or anything else that could be smoked. He stood outside the bathroom studying the placement of that object. *Hmm, I wonder if the beat guys or ETs saw that ashtray.* His curiosity roused, he carefully undid a portion of the police tape and entered Nicole's bedroom.

Chapter Twelve

Whirley didn't try to stay within the speed limit. "Don't you worry, hon, I'm not new at this."

"Great. But there's no reason to be setting speed records. Besides, won't the cops notice?"

She glanced towards him. "You see anyone else going the limit? At this time of night, it's the only way you don't get shot or carjacked. You do know Chicago's streets ain't the safest. We're on the West side."

"Yeah, I'd much rather be heading east and north."

She shot him another look. "I'm not an Uber or taxi service. Relax, you'll get your rocks off soon enough."

Jim squirmed in his seat. "About that…"

"What'samatter? You've turned prudish or something. You don't find me sexy? Honey, when we're done you won't know what world you've been in."

Jim gulped. "No, no it's not that. You're very…eh…attractive. It's just…well…out-of-the-blue."

"Life happens. Opportunity knocks and you either answer, or, baby, it's gone. You know what I mean?" She put her hand on his thigh and worked her way to his crotch. "Jimbo, I felt something move in there. It's rising to the occasion. Unlike the crap in your noggin, your dick does its own thinking." She laughed.

Jim also felt the sensation and she certainly knew what she was doing. He placed his hand on top of hers. "Why?"

"Why, what?" she asked as she rubbed the area.

"Why are you doing this? What about your old man and his boys?"

"Is that what's worrying you?"

Jim found it difficult to swallow. Caught between a tinge of fear mixed with guilt and the massaging of his dick, he was losing the battle. "Yeah, yes."

"Don't you worry, Jimbo, it will be all explained."

* * *

Neve took the exclusivity of her Gold Coast neighborhood in stride. She was used to a certain lifestyle along with the perks that came with it. Coming from a big old house on the outskirts of Savannah, Georgia, she had never wanted for money or anything else. Daddy always saw to it.

Her father made his fortune buying and selling companies, one of which happened to be in Chicago. His company owned the condo she lived in, but why go into a lot of detail. Easier to say, it's daddy's.

She did tell the officer the truth. The one who leered at her, Joe, she thought that was his name. But not the whole truth. She heard more than a thump. She heard a door slam and seconds later she heard it again. Then the unmistakable clank of the old elevator. She didn't know whether it was going up or down. She did what any curious dumb-ass girl would do…she peeked out her door and… well it looked like Jim in the cage, but it was dark and late, and God knows the amount of alcohol she consumed. Nikki, or as she was known professionally, Nicole, gossiped to her which guy was good and which…you know. Jim, she kept for safekeeping. Not bad, but useful in the office. This other man—Jesus, Nikki's eyes would go wide, and she'd salivate in front of Neve. She never said who this sexual magician was, but the sounds they made penetrated the thick walls and carpet of the building. She had a difficult time sleeping through those nights.

She was taken aback when the cops told her Nicole was dead, but not so surprised as to let on. No doubt, Nikki led a fast-paced life. Something she admired. How Nikki kept all the balls in the air—Neve smiled at the play on words—in the air was a tribute to

Nikki's drive as well as sexual appetite. She knew from Daddy that Nikki was a rising star. Her ability to promote and navigate in the board room, she was told, was like watching Paul McCartney play ten different instruments, perfectly.

Her daddy called her later in the day after the police found Nicole. He asked her to say as little as possible. She wouldn't do otherwise.

Chapter Thirteen

Jim stumbled onto the front porch of his house. He had no idea of the time, but believed it was close to sunrise. Whirley was true to her word—his world had changed. He squinted toward the brightening eastern sky and before facing Lori, tried to make sense of the last 24 or so hours.

His car ride with Whirley ended in front of a rehabbed two-flat. He wasn't sure if they were still in Chicago or a near western suburb. She ushered him in and unlocked the 2nd floor apartment door.

"Now you wash up in that bathroom in the master bedroom and get comfy. I'll use the one down the hall."

He kept telling himself that this couldn't be happening, and he should get out. But as Whirley acknowledged, his dick had other plans. He used the bathroom and took a quick shower. He got into bed, but at the last minute decided to at least have his underwear on, as stupid of a getaway plan his other head could muster.

Time seemed to standstill. Any sound from creaks to toilet flushing put him on edge. He was losing desire.

"I'll be there in a few more minutes," Whirley shouted from someplace in the apartment. "I want you ready and hot."

He looked around the sparsely furnished room. There were no pictures on the walls and the only other piece of furniture besides the large bed was a dresser. He should have checked the closet...too late. Whirley could come in at any moment. His member went into hiding as his anxiety grew with each passing second.

"I'm just putting on the finishing touches," Whirley said, "be there in a minute or two."

"Finishing touches?" What the hell? His imagination shoved his unease aside. Maybe, this never-happened-before-in-his-life, will actually take place.

He heard footsteps, then a figure appeared in the doorway.

"My, my, did you run out of places to go?" Lori said after she opened the front door of their house. "You better come in before the neighbors see. What the hell happened to you at the police station?"

Jim slowly made his way through the entryway. His mind, though, remained somewhere on the west side.

"Did the cops...?" Lori looked closer. "Where the hell were you?

He tried to dodge her but failed. She must have smelled the perfume by the angry look on her face.

"You piece of..."

Jim put his hand up to shield himself. "It's not what you think."

Lori stood with one hand on her hip. "What do I think?"

Jim didn't answer but made his way to the bar. He took a glass off the shelf and filled it halfway with bourbon, then drank. He felt the heat of the liquid pass his throat. It made him cough. When he regained control, he held his drink in his hand. "I got screwed," then took another gulp.

"That's it. That's all you're going to tell me. You got fucked." She knocked the drink from his hand and went after him with her fists. "You...you...how could...who..." She burst into tears.

He grabbed her hands and held them tightly. "It's...it's not what... Will you stop this shit and listen?"

* * *

Home was a block away as Neve returned from her second party in two nights. She had forgotten about the undercover car parked in front of her building. She was of no mind to look. She was high. Someone or something tugged on her sleeve.

"Where are we going?" the male voice giggled.

"Huh?" She glanced at the person.

"They said you are a rich Southern belle." His eyes swept the building, "Goddamn, I'm goin' to bag a Gold Coast baby. Sweet."

"You… bag…What did you say?" She screwed up her face. "Hey, you have blond hair. I like guys with blond…"

He grabbed her arm, pulling her closer. "Never mind what I said." He tried to stick his tongue in her mouth.

"Stop. What are you doing?"

"It's called kissing up here. Don't know what it's called where you come from."

She broke away from his grip. "Okay, hungry boy, try to catch me."

"If I do…?"

She smiled. "First you have to…" She took off. After a burst of speed, she glanced back.

He followed but tripped on his own feet. "Hey…"

"If you want it, you better…"She laughed. She got to the outside door of the building. Panting, she slung her purse to her front. *Where's the damn keys.* Her hands dug through the contents. She looked back and saw him gaining ground.

"I'm com'n. I'm bagg'n one Gold Coast baby tonight." His voice ricocheted off the stone and brick facades.

Shit. She stuck her hand in her pocket. *Keys, thank god.* She stole a sideway glance and saw he was loping up the front walk. Holding the key, she missed putting it into the lock. She heard his breathing not far behind. She went toward the keyhole again, but before the key found its mark, the door opened. "Fuck." She stumbled into a man.

"Neve?"

She backed away. "Do I know…?"

"Hey, get your hands off my…" The blond kid stopped in mid-sentence as the man pulled out some sort of ID.

"Detective Brandt. Homicide."

"Hom-i-… Naw you're fuck'n pull'n…" He shook Neve's shoulder. "Is he for real?"

"I guess." Her voice gave off the vibe of one not yet persuaded.

The blond kid pulled himself up to his full six-foot height. "I caught her, and you know what that means?" He rocked on his heels.

"It means you better get the hell out of here before you're cuffed and taken to the station."

"On what charge? We're just having… what are we having?"

"Okay, son. Call it a night. I'll get you an Uber."

"That's okay, Mister." He started to back down the walk. "It's all right. You can have her. She's some rich Southern b-bitch. Jesus I could have…I could have…"

"Nice friends you keep," Brandt said, as the kid disappeared.

"Not my friend. We…" She looked up at the ceiling for the words. "Oh yeah. Met at a party. He followed me home. I think. I don't even know his name." She giggled, then caught herself and pushed the button for the elevator. "Can I ask a question?"

"Sure."

"You a cop, right?"

"Yes, I'm a detective."

"Huh." She brushed some hair from her face and concentrated. She pointed at him. "Why are you here at this time of night? Day? Whatever?"

"You know the woman on the third floor was found dead?"

"Yeah, I was told. No one said she was murdered or anything." She took a breath and said more to herself, "Nikki dead. Holy shit." She tried to follow their conversation.

"True. We're not sure how Nicole died."

They heard the clang of the cage and watched its slow descent.

"Did you know Nicole?"

Neve shrugged. "Like I told the two out there, enough to say hi and bye. She seemed nice, polite, and…"

The elevator arrived. She pulled at the sliding gate to open. "Sonofabitch."

"Let me help." Brandt took hold of the handle. "There you go."

She stepped in as well as Brandt. He pressed 2.

"How did you know my floor? Oh, I get it. There're only three floors and…" She laughed. "Am I stupid."

The elevator moved slowly.

"Were you ever in Nicole's apartment?"

"Yeah, a few times. I mean, well, once or twice. She ran out of coffee or something."

"Uh-huh. Did Nicole smoke?"

"Smoke what?"

"Anything. Cigarettes, pot, whatever."

"Did Nicole smoke? Smoke." She shook her head. "No, definitely not. Not allowed." She broke out laughing again. "Can't do it in this building. Against the rules."

The elevator stopped moving. This time she had no trouble pulling the gate. "This is my stop." She gazed into Brandt's face. "But you already knew that. Have a nice night, or day, I'm going to bed."

"You too." Brandt watched as she struggled to unlock her front door. When she succeeded and was about to step into her apartment, he asked one more question. "What do you know about Jim?"

Chapter Fourteen

Detective Young came in early to check on the supplemental reports. She was a few steps into the general office space on the 2nd floor when she saw Brandt hovering by the coffee machine. She walked over and watched him for a few seconds.

"Hey Brandt, you look like you've been spun around in a washing machine." She picked out a can of diet cola from the fridge below the coffee maker. "Didn't you sleep?"

"Why, is my shirt on backwards or something?"

"No, but your hair is charging in different directions, and you forgot to shave."

"You have something against the rugged man look?"

She could have responded with a slight but held her tongue, ignoring his question. "Anything new on Nicole?"

"You mean has the autopsy come back?" He didn't wait for a response. "Why don't we step into my humble office, and I'll catch you up."

"Ooh, this sounds serious."

He grunted. "Suit yourself."

"Okay, okay. Jesus."

"He had nothing to do with it."

She followed him to his cubicle. "You're grumpy. What happened?" She pulled up a cheap plastic chair.

He got behind his desk and rummaged through a sheaf of papers. "Here it is, the medical examiner's statement." He handed it to her, then leaned back in his chair.

She went through the report. "She definitely had alcohol, but not nearly enough to kill her. The lab found no other drugs."

"Keep reading."

"No bullet entries, knife cuts, defensive wounds."

"Yeah, yeah, I'm aware. Get to the last page."

She flipped to the end. At the bottom under Cause of Death: she read, <u>UNDETERMINED</u>. "What the hell?"

"That's what I said."

Young reread the report. "Bullshit. Don't you think? Most people don't up and die, particularly someone who's young and in good health."

"Well, all we know is she's young. We'll have to get her medical records and that will take time."

"Damn." She moved closer. "What does your gut say, Brandt? No foul play?"

He rubbed his chin. "Shit, I did forget to shave." He stood and walked around his desk. "I think... I think there's things to investigate. Last night, I went back to the scene."

She straightened in her chair. "You did, without me?"

He shrugged. "It was on my way home."

Her eyes narrowed and she screwed her mouth into a smirk.

"Anyway, I ran into the second-floor neighbor, Neve something. She knows more than she's telling. I'm sure of it."

"Like what?"

"Her relationship with Nicole for one as well as our person of interest, Jim."

"Okay, what else?"

"I found something in Nicole's apartment. An ashtray. It was full. I took it to the lab on my way to work."

"What's the deal with that?"

"It could lead to who else was there before or after Jim. Nicole was a very giving woman."

"Sexist."

"Just reporting the facts, ma'am."

She gazed at the ceiling, then at him. "Did you go into Nicole's bedroom?"

"Yeah, I did."

"Did you find a snifter by the bed? Williams, the beat officer, mentioned it in his report."

He thought for a moment. "No, I didn't come across it. It could be at the lab?"

"Let's hope so. I better find Williams."

* * *

It was not quite daybreak and Whirley was very pleased with herself. She stood in the doorway in her wig of down-to-her-shoulders blonde hair, wearing nothing more than a string bra and a thong that showed off her assets. Jimbo was ready to be plucked. She moved slowly toward the bed. His gaze was rapture-like. Whatever anxiety, guilt, or negative feelings the chump had went…puff. He couldn't take his eyes off her. As she neared the bed, he reached out, but she pushed him away. She was a prick teaser supreme; her hand lightly touched his chest, running her fingers down his stomach, then played with the waist band of his very tighty whities. The result she witnessed was a tent pole down there. She heard him sigh, then he tried to grab her breast, which she deflected. "Patience," then pointed to his underwear. He didn't need to be asked twice. He quickly disposed of them. His glory stood at a hard salute. She undid her bra and watched him salivate. She had a great rack, and he bucked a little when he saw them unbound. She told him to slow down. She inched her breasts close to his mouth, but before he could kiss or lick them, pulled away. "Nice boy. We're going to have fun." She moved down his body and got between his legs, her mouth almost touching his pole. She grabbed the beast. But before he could enjoy her hold, she heard footsteps, then saw a flash of light.

"Okay, Whirley, you did good. Get your ass out of here for a few minutes. There's business to discuss with…"

"Jimbo?"

The large man with the camera and a smile on his face nodded. "Yeah, him."

She started to get up.

"Wait, one more picture with your tongue on his dick."

She looked. "Where did it go?" and laughed. "Sure." Her hand did the trick, and the flash went off. She got up and as she walked past the man, he slapped her backside. "You have good taste, Jimbo. A fine piece of ass, if I say so myself."

* * *

Jim's memory of the last several hours flashed by as he held Lori until her crying turned into whimpers. "You want Kleenex?"

She nodded and went to the couch and curled into a fetal position.

"Here." He handed her a box and waited. She sat up, then blew her nose.

He watched, then took a deep breath and hoped he had the strength to get through the next few minutes. "Before you say anything more, or think god knows what, I'll tell you straight out I fucked up both with Nicole and what happened last night."

He placed his hand on top of hers. She let it stay.

"First, I didn't kill anyone." He paused. "Without getting into details that will only…well, Nicole was very much alive when I left her."

She looked away and withdrew her hand.

"Lori, please, I'm not trying to hurt you anymore than I did. Nicole and I happened." He shrugged. "I'm sorry."

If she had lasers for eyes, her gaze would have cut through him.

"We'll get back to that part," she said. "Tell me about last night."

Jim stood and paced in front of her. "A woman picked me up when I was released from the police station. She said we'd go for a drink. I didn't see the harm."

"Let me guess, you ended up…"

"No, no, we …" He took a deep breath. "She drove me to some place on the West side or Western suburb. When we got there, she led me to a room in the apartment."

Lori's eyes welled with tears. "You...you... tell me you didn't. Please God..."

"Don't get so dramatic." Jim's mouth went dry. He needed another drink. "I'll be right..." and pointed to the bar. His hand shook slightly as he took another glass. "You want some?" Hearing no response, he poured the bourbon into his tumbler, then gulped down half of it. He returned to the couch and sat next to her. He reached out for her with his free hand, but she inched away. The drink sloshed up the sides from his tremor. He started to speak, stopped, then tried again. "Here goes... I'm being blackmailed."

"You what? Black... what the hell are you talking about? Look at me, Jim O'Dell. I don't want to hear any more bullshit—the truth for once in your goddamn life." She stood over him and grabbed his glass, downing the rest of the drink.

He tried to stay calm, but a deep tiredness came over him. The strain of the last 48 hours caught up. "Believe me or not," he said slowly, "but there is a lot more going on at our office than you or I ever dreamed."

Chapter Fifteen

Neve stared at the snifter she retrieved from Nicole's apartment. One would think with the cops around, she would have had a difficult time getting into Nicole's place. Instead, it was wicked easy. Neve waited until all the police trooped out, counted to fifty, then took the stairs armed with her cell phone's flashlight and Nicole's spare key. All she had to do was not tear the "DO NOT ENTER" tape. She knew the layout of Nicole's place well, having been there many times, even partied with Nicole and Jim on several occasions. What bothered her was Nicole's tight lips about the other guy—the sex magician. Not a word of description about his looks, his age, or where they'd met. Only about what he did for her in bed, rather, what they did together.

On that night or morning when Nicole was found dead, Neve had stayed by her door after viewing the elevator descend. After a minute or so there was a thump. She played with the lock but heard nothing else. Given her state of alcohol consumption and a few blunts, maybe it was her imagination. She left her front door slightly ajar and went to the kitchen for a drink. She was tired from that first party but not enough for sleep. She grabbed a book and casually picked at a school assignment. School was boring as hell, but the social side of things kept her interest. She wasn't nearly as active as she believed Nikki was, but then again Nikki had a few years on her. She got through maybe a page or was it three? Her mind wandered, thinking about Jim and the mystery man, when she heard sirens. She watched through the crack of her front door the police comings and goings, waiting until the building quieted. If the police thought there was foul play, they didn't follow much of the protocols she had seen on TV. She wasn't overcome with fear or sadness for her now deceased friend. Somehow, she wasn't all that surprised. She went to her front window and saw the police and ambulance pull away. *Jesus, Nikki, you shit.* A smile came over her. Now was her chance to satisfy her curiosity about the mysterious him—find a letter, or photo.

After quiet returned to the building, Neve snuck up the stairs to Nicole's. The spare key worked awesomely. Inside the apartment, the cops appeared not to have moved a thing. The living room/dining room was as spotless as usual. Nicole rarely entertained in that manner. To her, indoor dining had a very different meaning. In the kitchen, Neve went through several drawers and shelves where notes could have been kept but found nothing. She then went down the hallway leading to Nikki's bedroom. Police tape blocked the entrance. Neve thought about her next move, then removed one side and shimmied her way in. She went to the nightstand and was about to reach for the drawer handle when she spotted an edge of a clear plastic something sticking out from behind a leg of the table. She grabbed it. Inside the clear bag was a brandy glass. She was up on the latest TV cops shows and reasoned the cops bagged it for evidence…maybe it had someone's DNA. She inspected the bag again, holding it up to the light coming from a window. She considered herself a petite connoisseur of wine and noticed the drying legs on the side of the glass. She hadn't decided what to do with it when she heard voices coming towards her. *Shit.* She held onto the package and raced to Nicole's walk-in closet, closing the door as the voices and footsteps neared the room.

"Hey, the tape blocking the bedroom fell. Jesus, can't the beat guys do anything right?" The voice had a distinct Chicago male accent.

"Forget about it. We're here for the evidence envelope. Williams said he left it on the nightstand." The tone was unaccented and male.

Neve opened the door a crack.

"Where did Williams say it was?"

"Nightstand."

"Unless I've gone blind, there's nothing here," A short, stubby man with a cigar hanging from his mouth moved the few books that rested on top. Still searching, he dropped to his knees. "Noth'n down here or behind the table," He leaned on the bed to stand.

"Not the first time the beat guys screwed up," a taller, older man said. "Let me think. Check the other side closest to the closet."

Neve stepped back from the door. The men were very close.

"Nada. Jesus. Say, is this Williams guy a nut or a joker?"

"What about the closet?" Neve was certain that was the cigar guy.

"Why would Williams put evidence in the closet when we heard him say nightstand?"

"Beats the hell out of me," Cigar guy's voice easily penetrated the closet door. "Maybe it rolled there by accident."

"Put on gloves before you touch the handle."

"What for? We already screwed up."

A ray of light from the bedroom lit the closet. The cigar man was within a few feet of Neve who hid behind several hung coats. From what she saw, the man was concentrating on the floor.

"Hell of a lot of shoes." He closed the door. "Hey Harry, what is it about women and shoes. My wife is the same. I've got two pair. Who would need more than that?"

"You're not a woman. Let's get out of here. One of the beat guys must have taken it."

* * *

Brandt moved his landline office phone over to where Det. Young sat. "Dial Williams' number."

Young picked up the receiver and stopped. "Damnit, I don't know it." She had an "excuse-me" expression on her face.

"Call the desk downstairs."

She gave him a "you must think I'm stupid" look, then punched the three-digit number for internal information. The desk sergeant gave her the number and she made the call.

Williams picked up after several rings. "Yeah, Williams here."

"Williams, this is Detective Young, out of Grand and Central. Your report on the Nicole McMaster matter indicated you found a snifter by Nicole's bed. Did you inventory it and take it to the lab?"

There was a pause on the line. "The glass by her bed? Yeah, I bagged it, then got busy with other things and forgot to take it. I told the ET guys to pick it up."

"The ET…do you remember who?"

"Hold on. I'll check my phone."

Young covered the mouthpiece and told Brandt what was going on.

"Yeah, Detective?"

"I'm here.

"Here's the number. His first name is Harry don't know his last."

"Got it."

She hung up with Williams and dialed the number. She introduced herself after the call was answered.

"Nah, never found it," Harry said, "my partner and I looked all over for the damn thing. We thought Williams must have taken it to the lab."

"You're kidding?"

"No ma'am. We searched the place pretty good, but there was no snifter. Ask Williams."

"I did. He didn't take it either," and she hung up.

Young was about to relay to Brandt what had transpired.

"I heard enough to know." He pretended to sift through some papers.

"Let's go back there. Things like that don't disappear into thin air."

Brandt looked up. "You haven't worked here long enough but I'll go anyway."

Chapter Sixteen

Carla wondered if she got home too late for Brandt. After the night she had, it would have been a relief to be with him. She returned to her apartment around 4 a.m. but it could have been earlier or later. She was not one concerned with exact time. She stowed her long blonde wig alongside many others deep within her closet, well out of sight from curious eyes.

If one were to ask her occupation, she'd answer actress, or social worker. She played both. She could transform herself like a chameleon, accents and all. Others would describe her as a lady of the evening, even though on most occasions she used sex as bait. From time to time, she would put out, if necessary.

Take last night as an example. Her assignment was to pickup a Jim O'Dell from the police station and entice him. She showed up dressed in tight jeans and a jacket that revealed just enough. It was all the persuasion he needed to get into her car. Why her people wanted him, she didn't know, nor did she want to know. She did her job. She had him, according to the phrase, "eating out of her hand," although she was sure Jimbo was concentrating on other parts. The shock on Jimbo's face when the pictures were taken was as good as getting paid—at least for the moment. She left the poor chump in their hands and went home with a pocketful of cash. She got compensated well.

Brandt was a different story. Yeah, they met at a bar about a month ago. She wasn't there because he was the mark. Like Cole Porter wrote, "it was just one of those things." As she remembered it was late, near last call. She had been sitting and chatting with the bartender, Dino. Given the frequency of her visits, they had become acquainted.

Bartenders, like many fishermen, had great stories. In much the same way her occupation gave her a lifetime of stories, a bartender also had a unique perch from which to watch life unfold. Their qualifications were similar: be a good listener, feign compassion, and know when to shut up and when to give advice. The main difference between them was the sex part, but she was sure he got offers too.

Dino was in the middle of one of his tales, getting close to the punchline, when this unshaven gruff-looking guy pulled up a bar stool and sat next to her. He didn't say a word. He put his drink down and gave Dino his full attention—as if what Dino was saying was the most remarkable story he'd ever heard. When Dino finished, the stranger lifted his glass in a toast and asked if he could buy Carla a drink. Who was she to refuse? Besides, it was late and one for the road wouldn't hurt anybody. Dino hung around a few minutes, making sure the new guy wasn't up to no good, then he drifted into the background.

She learned her new companion went by Brandt and she gave hers as Carla. It was a momentary inspiration, having used so many different ones. There were times her memory lapsed as to her true Christian name. They shared a few laughs and another drink or two. Then he helped her out the door. He asked if he could call. His question was quite a change of pace from the usual. She hid her smile and wondered if he was playing her. As the evening went on, she became convinced he wasn't. What washed over her was something she hadn't felt in a long while…real.

During their long walk, she explained in not so many words that she worked odd hours. He nodded and said he did too. Neither she nor he spelled out what they did. They agreed the less said the better. Camelot wasn't perfect either.

* * *

"Blackmail?" Lori repeated the word. "That's the lamest fuck'n excuse for fucking around I've ever heard. Was that after your orgasm or before the whore got hers? What the hell do you take me for? A fool? A scared little bitch? Jesus, Jim." She got up from the couch and began to pace. Abruptly, she stopped. "We're at a crossroads and it's time to assess. You obviously want someone other than me. I don't know when or why things have gone south but we both can agree it has."

Jim opened his mouth, then stopped. He put his hand up. "You're not listening. Forget the sex, the screwing. Mea culpa, I'm totally to blame, but Lori, these people don't play around."

Lori stood over Jim. "Whatta you talking about? What people?"

He shook his head. "Damn it, you haven't been listening except for the sex part. Sex was a ruse to get me to an apartment." He swallowed hard. "They... eh... took... pictures... compromising ones."

Lori's face reddened and her jaw dropped. "W..h..a...t? There're naked pictures of you with a whore? Jesus, shit, how could..." She choked on the words. "You're... you... I can't even find the words."

"Call me disgusting, but there's a bigger picture."

"Uh-huh, bigger idiot, fool, asshole...." She fought to control herself. "I need space. I need to... Can you get the hell out of here? How can I...we... show our face at... You will have cost us our jobs. We'll be out of work. We'll lose the house... everything. You dumb ass shit." Her whole body shook, like a huge electric shock went through her. "Get out—get your stuff and move out."The words came out in a defiant growl.

Jim watched Lori's performance, part of him surprised, the other acknowledging what he guessed would be coming. It still stunned him, especially the anger. He hadn't seen that much passion from her since... he didn't know when. He slowly got up. They stood within inches of each other. "Lori, I'm trying to warn you. Goddamn it." His preaching had no effect. She was stone-faced. "Okay, you're doing your usual of focusing on the trees and not the forest. My going accomplishes nothing. We have to—"

She slapped him across his face. "Get the fuck out."

Instinctively he raised his hand. She flinched. Instead of striking her, he rubbed his cheek and after a moment said, "Bitch, I'm out of here. I'll get a few things and leave."

She stepped out of his way as he went to the bedroom. He retrieved a suitcase from the closet and packed his clothes. Thank God, he had a spare phone. It didn't take him long. She hadn't moved from the couch area as he went to the front entrance. He wagged his forefinger at her. "You'll regret this. Don't think these same people won't come after you. They will." He opened the door and wheeled the suitcase to the porch. He'd wait for a cab outside, as the police still had his car. Ten minutes later, a multi-colored vehicle drove up. The driver rolled down his window.

"You called for a cab?"

Jim shaded his eyes. He caught a glimpse of the driver, hesitated for a moment, then headed to the back of the vehicle. The cabbie popped the trunk, and Jim dropped the luggage. He then got into the back seat.

"Airport?"

"No, no airport. Take me to…" Jim fingered his phone… "Schiller and Astor."

"Gold Coast…hmm."

"Anything wrong?"

"Nope, not a thing."

Chapter Seventeen

"I'll drive," Young said to Brandt. "You can take a nap on the ride over to Nicole's."

"I look that bad?"

"Honey, I've seen cadavers look better."

Brandt reached for his jacket. "Okay, dead man walking." As soon as they got into her car, Brandt closed his eyes. "Wake me when we get there."

"Anything else? Coffee, doughnuts? I'm full service."

He opened an eye and thought of a quip but decided she could take it the wrong way. "Nah, driving is good enough." He raised his thumb to signify agreement. She pulled out of the parking lot, and he drifted off.

The car stopped. "We're here," she said.

He raised his head. "What? How long have I been asleep—five minutes?"

"It was forty. You missed all the fun traffic."

"I'll make it up to you on the way back." He unhooked his seat belt and opened the car door. Getting out, he stretched. "Feel better all ready. That's the building, the brownstone in the middle of the block."

He saw Young shade her eyes. "Looking for something?"

"Yeah, no security outside the place?"

Brandt shrugged. "It's not necessarily a homicide investigation. Remember? The autopsy doesn't say."

"R-i-i-i-g-h-t," she said. "Shall we?"

They walked into the building. Brandt remarked it might be faster to take the stairs. He pointed to the elevator. "As you can see, this contraption was in vogue back in the nineteen-twenties. It's not what one would call a speedster, but it's ornate."

They compromised. They'd take the ride up and the stairs on the return. Brandt was right. It was a slow ascent along with complementary clanging. They reached the third floor. Brandt pulled back the black metal gate. He and Young stepped out and stood in front of Nicole's door.

"Someone forgot to re-tape the door." Young held onto the freed side of the yellow tape, as Brandt took the key out of his case folder.

"Nicole, as you will soon see, lived well." He guided the key into the lock and opened the door. "Voilà, enter her mini palace."

* * *

Neve opened her apartment door. She wore a man's shirt that went past her hips. Her hair was uncombed, and she wore no makeup.

"What the fuck are you doing here?" Neve asked as Jim wheeled his suitcase into her condo. She put her hand on her hip as he walked past her.

"Whatta you mean? Isn't this what you wanted? You sent me tons of messages pleading that we should be together. Well, here I—" He heard the clamor of the elevator and looked toward the opened door. "Close it, damn. No wait, go see."

Neve didn't move.

"P-l-e-a-s-e," he whispered, tone harsh.

It must have gotten her out of her stupor. She hurried to her entrance and closed the door enough to peek. "It's that cop from yesterday with a bitch. Must be his partner or something." Her tone was in between a whisper and normal as she glanced back at Jim.

He motioned for her to shut the door.

She waited a second or two. They both heard the unmistakable sound of the motor whine as it took the cage to the third floor, giving way to the metal screech of the sliding gate.

"Shit, why are they here?" Jim paced, then stopped. "Listen, they'll be coming down here…I know." He glanced around her apartment and focused on her bedroom. "Do you mind?"

"Huh?"

"Your room. Can we go there?"

"You and me? I… I'm yucky. Look at me. I haven't taken a shower. I just got up, besides I'm not in the mood to jump your bones."

"Me neither." He shifted his weight. "It wouldn't be good for either of us if those cops found me with you. They already think I may have had something to do with Nicole's death."

"Did you?"

"No…not at all. She was… never mind. Let's talk in there."

* * *

Nicole's apartment was in the same condition as when Brandt left it. Nothing seemed out of order. They walked through the front to the kitchen and then the hallway leading to the bedrooms.

"Where did you find that ashtray you photographed?" Young asked.

"The bathroom, it was behind the toothbrushes on the vanity."

"Strange place for that, don't you think?"

Brandt pointed to the spot. "Yeah, since according to the neighbor Neve, smoking was *verboten* in the building."

"Did you check out the medicine cabinet?"

Brandt stroked his chin. "No, I missed it."

"Let's look."

Young slid the mirrored panel to the three-shelf cabinet. "Holy crap, that girl had a drug store in here." She reached for a few of the bottles. Young examined the labels: Annandatol, Buspirone XL, Rexulti, Nardil, among others. Many of the bottles were prescribed by different doctors.

Brandt examined the medicines too. "These are for anti-depressants and anxiety." He scratched his head. "Too much sex and rock and roll for the poor girl to cope."

Young shot him a disapproving look. "You don't know that. I'll take pictures of all the bottles. At least we know the doctors to contact."

"Okay. Take the pictures." He waited until Young finished, then grabbed as many of the bottles he could and squeezed them into his jacket pocket. He then led the way to Nicole's bedroom. "I'll tell you what's strange," he said, pulling the police tape to the side, "with all those drugs, the autopsy didn't find any in her body."

"Interesting. Here's another. Jim said he brought Champagne. Where's the bottle?"

Brandt agreed and began to look under the bed and behind the nightstand. "Besides dust balls, there's nothing here…no bottle or brandy glass."

Young checked out the closet. "Same here, although a hell of a lot of shoes and clothes."

They stood in the middle of the spacious room. "Where do we go from here?" Young asked.

Brandt looked around. "Let's check out her glassware."

"Glassware, why?"

Young, followed Brandt out but stopped to rehang the tape. They then trooped down the hallway, through the kitchen, and into the dining room.

The china cabinet was a formidable piece dressed in dark wood with lighted glass shelves. On the first two shelves were expensive dishes and platters. The third had assorted glassware.

"Count the wine and liquor glasses," Brandt said.

"There's eight of each."

"And brandy snifters."

"Let's see." Young moved some of the pieces. "I count three."

They looked at each other. Brandt cleared his throat, "Three huh, imagine that. Take pictures, then let's go. On the way down we'll stop by Neve and see if her memory is better than the night before."

Young snapped the photos, then closed the cabinet. She rubbed her thumb and forefinger together. "There's dust on the glasses. Doubt if they'd been used in a while."

Brandt stood by the front entrance. "Nothing like doing a puzzle. Only we don't know how many pieces the damn thing is missing." He waited for Young to exit, then locked the door and refixed the tape. "After you, Madam." He checked the time. "Ms. Neve may just be getting up, considering how zonked she was last night. This should be a trip."

Chapter Eighteen

onavan Hill was of average height. He was a grey man in a gray suit. The kind of person eyes didn't notice. He wasn't an intellectual or a man who spent his time contemplating worldly matters. He was loyal to his work and the purpose for it. Few knew of him and even fewer had any idea of the group he headed. His unit didn't appear on any corporate chart or have a listed phone number. It was always Mr. Hill to those who worked for him.

Whirley and Jim weren't the only ones who drove to the apartment in Bellwood that night. Mr. Hill was there too, although after arriving he chose to sit in his parked car biding his time. His wait lasted about thirty minutes before his phone buzzed.

"Mr. Hill, all's clear. Everything worked like a charm."

Hill recognized the voice. "The mark is gone?"

"Yes sir."

"And the girl?"

"She left too."

He disconnected and got out of his car. The collar of his raincoat, although there was no rain or snow, shielded the lower part of his face. His hat did most of the rest. He walked up the stairs of the building and gave the signal. He knocked twice paused, then again on the apartment door. Joe, a huge hunk of a middle-aged man who went by the street name, Skinny, answered.

"Right this way, Mr. Hill. The pictures are in the bedroom."

Hill grunted, took his hat off, lowered his collar, then followed.

"The photos came out real good. The broad was a pro."

"Yeah? We've used her before?"

"Yes sir…a few times."

"What does she know?"

"Just what we tell her. She keeps her nose clean and mouth shut."

Hill looked at the pictures. "Not in this one she don't."

Skinny laughed. "That's a good one, Mr. Hill."

Hill didn't smile. "Why isn't she fucking him?"

Skinny swallowed. "I…I…that wasn't in the orders."

Hill glanced at his underling, then the pictures. "It'll do. Next time at least have her on top and the mark's hands on her ass. *Capishe?*"

"Yes sir."

He slipped the pictures in his coat pocket and stepped toward the door. "How many times have we used the broad?"

"Eh…not…have to check our records."

Hill drew himself up. "More than three?"

Skinny nodded. "Yeah, I'm pretty sure. Off the top of my head I'd say at least ten."

"Ten! Jesus, too many, way too many. Shit." Hill tapped his jaw with his fingers. A smile crept over his face. "How long have you been with us, Skinny?

"Me? Well, I don't know…awhile."

"Awhile, huh, you're modest Skinny. The boss loves you. Ever since he thought of buying the company, he thinks you've done a fine job."

"Thanks, Mr. Hill. I think the boss is great, too."

Hill moved closer and in a low tone of voice asked him if he ever… and made a crude gesture.

Skinny's eyes nearly popped out of their sockets. "No sir, no sir. I don't, I wouldn't… touch… There's strict rules about that kind of stuff."

"But you'd want to if you could?"

"Hell yeah. She's a fine piece of ass, excuse the language, Mr. Hill, but God almighty, it would be a night to remember."

"I thought so. Here's the deal. In the next week or two, take her out and she's yours to do as you wish. When you're done, make sure she'll be a lasting memory."

Skinny rubbed his face.

Hill patted him on his shoulder. "You're a good man, Skinny, and you should reap the reward. These pictures will go a long way to destroy our mark's career as well as his wife's—I mean live-in girlfriend. Human Resources will have a field day as well as the cops."

Skinny wrinkled his face. "Sorry about Nicole. She was a nice girl."

Hill removed his hand from Skinny's shoulder. He put his hat back on and turned up his collar. "Yeah, she was, but a bad influence. Her ambition was... I can't say more, Skinny. The less you know, the better. Contact me when that broad is off the books."

* * *

Lori heard the door shut as Jim left. She stood near the couch and didn't move. She waited until a horn beeped, then stepped to the front entrance. She fought the desire to peek, and instead listened to bits of conversation. A car door closed, then the sound of a vehicle accelerating seeped through. No longer constrained, she opened the door and stepped onto the porch. *Holy shit.* She saw the rear end of the multicolored cab. *It couldn't be.* She watched as the car disappeared. *How many crazy-colored taxis are there?* She took a deep breath and walked back into the house. She had told Jim to put in deadbolts, but he never did. Instead, she slid the skimpy chain across the frame, then double-locked the door. *Could be a different driver.* The thought consoled her. Besides, what were the odds? What were... there were other things to think about... like getting through the rest of the day, then the next morning at her job.

She thought of calling her friends, Stacy or Tom. They were with her and Jim at dinner when Nicole phoned. She looked at her watch. It was already mid-morning. Her friends must have seen or read the news of what happened. *Wouldn't they be concerned? At the very least, gossip about it.* She eyed her cell. It displayed no messages or calls. *Shit.* She felt herself descending into the "woe is me" basement. *What did I do to deserve this?* If Jim was screwing Nicole, who else? How long? Why was she blind and didn't catch on?

Her house was so silent. Even her footsteps made no sound. She could drink the rest of the bottle Jim started. Drown herself into a boozy haze. She could…her phone went off. She nearly dropped it from the abruptness of the intrusion.

"H-e-l-l-o…Jim? Is that you, Jim?"

Chapter Nineteen

Neve followed Jim into her bedroom. She rubbed her eyes and yawned, "I'm still half asleep. I don't know why you're here and...."

"Neve, baby, remember all those good times...me, you and Nicole, and that other babe, what was her name?"

She swept her hair from her eyes and crinkled her nose. Her unbuttoned shirt left little to the imagination. A smile crossed her face, then quickly disappeared. "Cut the crap. You were going to tell me about Nicole. How do I know you didn't kill her?"

Jim frowned. "Why on earth would I? This..." He drew a circle in the air with his arm. "...was like a... What was that?"

"Huh? I didn't hear anything."

Jim lurched toward the bedroom entrance. "Listen...your front door." A knock echoed down the hallway.

She glanced around the room. "You're freaking me out. Hey, all this..." She shook her head. "Not my jam. I think you better...."

"There it is again. It's the cops. I know it. They're at your door."

"So? They don't know I'm home."

He ran his hand over his face. "Nah, that's no good. They'll come back. Go. I'll stay here." He looked toward the walk-in closet and pointed. "There, if I must. Now go."

She didn't move. He was within a foot or two from her. "Neve, do it." The words came out guttery, demanding. Her eyes widened, then she shrugged, giving the impression it was no big deal. She turned and went to answer. Jim had difficulty taking his eyes off her. Her gait was almost hypnotic. "Go, damn it, before they kick your door down."

* * *

Brandt and Young stood outside Neve's apartment. Brandt knocked politely. They listened for any sounds and after waiting several seconds, he did it with authority. "Neve, this is Detective Brandt, are you in there?" His question was met with silence. He shrugged. "I have a feeling the little lady is sleeping it off. We'll have to try her later." Brandt turned towards the stairs but stopped when he heard a click. He spun around and saw the door opened a crack.

"Who's there?

"We met last night or should I say early morning…Detective Brandt. My partner Detective Young is with me."

The space between the door and the jamb inched wider with enough room to see Neve's face.

"We'd like to chat."

"Chat?" Her eyebrows rose. "I just woke up. What time is it anyway?"

Brandt was within speaking distance of her. He rested his hand on the door and gently pushed it wider. "It's afternoon. Time to start the day."

"Hey, what are you doing?"

Brandt could now see into the apartment. He took in that Neve was dressed in a man's shirt, not buttoned, and presumably nothing else.

"Nice of you to invite us in." He pressed the door open and moved forward, forcing Neve to step back into the foyer.

"Hey, I didn't invite you. Get—"

"Neve, calm down. All we want to do is talk…better here than at the station."

"Station? Why? I didn't do nothing."

Brandt motioned Young to step in with him. "I believe without looking too hard my partner would find something here you're not supposed to have."

"I'm almost naked for God's sake. Don't you have manners?"

"I'm sure my partner and I are not offended by your undress."

"Stop. I don't… I'm calling Daddy." She stepped back into the apartment. "Where the hell is my phone?"

Brandt and Young were now in the middle of the vestibule. They watched her rummage the front part of the apartment. "My guess is the cell is in the bedroom." Brandt took a step forward to the border of the living room.

Neve looked up, her face flushed. "Bedroom?" She looked in that direction. Anyone could see inside. Her face reddened. "I…I…don't…shit, man, what's it your business where my phone is. Leave…Goddammit. I already told you all I know."

"Not everything," Brandt kept some space between them. "Did you have a key to Nicole's apartment?"

"A key? W…h…a…t?" Her eyes flickered upward, then recovered. "Yeah…once. She took it back. She got pissed at me for something."

"So, you don't have her key now?" Young joined in.

"No, I just said that. But if I did, I wouldn't even know where to look."

Brandt gave her an I-don't-believe-a-word-you're-saying, stare. "When was the last time you saw the key?"

Neve held the sides of her shirt together. "I don't keep track. I'm not sure she gave it back. It could be anywhere or nowhere."

Young was now in the living room moving toward the bedroom.

"Hey, where the fuck are you going?" Neve didn't wait for her answer. "You can't go in there. Stop." Young ignored Neve's protest.

"Where the…is my phone?" She glared at Young and let out a breath. "Screw you all." Young entered the bedroom.

"Look all you want." Neve searched for her cell in the living room, tossing pillows and seat coverings. Then got on the floor to look under the couch. She gave Brandt a full view of her partially covered ass. Not finding her cell, she got up. She was breathing heavy. "Okay, last warning. I want both of you out of here. My daddy is an important man. You'll have hell to pay."

Brandt smiled. "No problem. I also know many clout-heavy people. Just be straight with us, Neve, and we'll be out of your hair."

Young at that moment returned from the bedroom. "Forget the key. Couldn't find it." she said. "What about Jim?"

Chapter Twenty

Lori waited on the phone for several seconds after it rang. She heard breathing but no words. "Jim? You're scaring the shit out of me. Say something, Goddammit. Hello?" She moved the cell from her ear and looked at the screen. She didn't recognize the number, hesitated, then punched the Disconnect button. "Jesus." She sank back onto her couch and eyed the bottle of bourbon. What if it was that crazy cab driver? She reached for the booze, then hesitated. She gazed around the room. The quiet intensified…oppressive and unnerving. Think it out. The call could have been one of those Nigerian prince calls or some other bogus ones. That long-haired beast of a man wouldn't dare. She could have him fired… or worse.

She grabbed the bottle and held onto it. The sound of her heartbeat added to the depressive silence. She ran her tongue over her dry lips. "Damn," she said loudly, then left the bourbon where it was. As alluring as a drink would be, it wouldn't quell her pain. She realized drinking for what it was—a cheap bandage that would last only as long as the taste. She sighed. "Goddamn him." The sound of her voice smacked her back into reality.

What the hell. She threw Jim out for a reason. Why should she hang onto the possibility he'd call? She continued to make her case. It didn't take a genius to conclude he was the one who really walked out on the relationship. Telling him to leave was a tardy display, since he had already left months ago.

Would she take him back? The son of a bitch was a liar and a cheat. She could maybe live with that. But the worst sin of all was his betrayal of her trust. Flings can happen but carrying on a secret relationship was a fuck too far.

No drinks for her unless it was congratulatory. It was her second good decision of the day. Forcing Jim to leave was her first.

The pity party was over. She had to act. To confine herself to the damn house wouldn't solve the mystery of Nicole's death. Besides, somebody planted that jewelry in her car. Someone wanted her out of the way.... maybe it was Jim. She took a deep breath. Jim? How low could he go? But if it wasn't him, then there were other players...someone unseen, unnoticed. Perhaps Jim's story wasn't all that crazy.

The building where she worked would be empty on a Sunday. It was an opportunity to sniff around Jim's office and if her luck and courage held ...Nicole's.

* * *

Donavan Hill gazed out his small window of his inconspicuous office. It was hidden by an alcove in the corner of the third floor the company occupied. Sunday afternoons were usually quiet. The empty offices allowed him time to reflect and plan, then make his report to the Boss.

The Bears game played on his radio in the background. He'd catch the score now and then and gathered the Bears were about to lose another one.

He glanced at his desk. The photos taken of Jim and the girl were in color and left nothing to the imagination. Skinny was right about the bitch. She was hot. A small part of him sympathized with the chump. A smile crossed his face as he held one of the photos to the light. "Hard to refuse that." He dropped the picture and rubbed his eyes. When he was younger, he used to take delight in catching those who thought themselves above the rules. He'd get a real kick as they blubbered excuses and pleaded not to be exposed. That was when he was more of a freelancer and before he met the Boss.

Fifteen years he figured he'd been with JK and his various companies. JK had the morals of a junk bond salesman combined with the savviness and smarts of a Warren Buffett. One of his basic rules was to stay out of the limelight. If he'd walked into this

81

building, few would know him. However, many had felt his power and some, his wrath. There was little middle ground with him. Either you were 100% on his team or... Hill grunted at the thought.

JK had an innate sense about him. He could smell ambition in a person and was a master at stoking it, playing with it like a cat did a mouse. He'd delight in watching their eagerness for power and success grow, until it became overwhelming. He knew how to play into the victim's blindness. They never saw what was coming. That was where Hill came in. So far, he and JK were successful, and Hill worked to keep it that way.

Hill reviewed the photos again. He was sure the Boss would approve. After that...well, the chump and his live-in would be ruined. He checked the time. The Boss expected his call at precisely 12:47. He unlocked his desk drawer as well as the phone case and retrieved a mobile phone. The number Hill punched changed on a weekly basis. Despite the area code, he didn't know JK's location. He dialed and heard the connection.

"Good afternoon, sir. I have the photos. Everything went as planned."

"I'll have a look. I'll text your personal mobile where to drop them off. If they are as good as you say, distribute them as scheduled. I'll notify you later after receipt."

"Yes, sir. What about Nicole's office?"

"Ah, Nicole...poor girl. Any more news as to how it happened? Police say anything?"

"No sir, not yet."

"Hmm. Have the cops come by?"

"Not that I'm aware."

"Then there's no hurry. Make sure her office is secured."

Hill understood what that meant. "I'll check on it before I leave."

"Good. Anything else I should know about?"

"Things seem to be in control."

"That's when I worry. What about Neve? Is she upset about Nicole?"

Hill stared out the window. Neve? Why would JK care? He rarely spoke about her. He cleared his throat. "I'll look in on her, sir and report back."

"Thank you, Mr. Hill."

The line went dead. Hill re-cased the cell and locked it, then the drawer. He scooped the photos from his desk and dropped them in the envelope Skinny gave him. He could walk the three flights to Nicole's office or use the elevator. He took his coat and decided to get a little exercise and climb the stairs.

* * *

Lori flashed her ID badge at the guard on duty as she entered the building. She didn't recognize the graying Black man who manned the control desk. A polite smile stretched her lips while she waited. "Hope the afternoon is going well," she said.

He looked up for a second from his small TV and waved her through the security apparatus leading to the bank of elevators. He didn't say a word, much less a second glance.

Her heart pounded as she waited. Should she go through with it? There was still the option of leaving. The guard could care less. She looked at the monitor that tracked the particular elevator. It would be here in a second or two. *Shit.* She bit her lip. A soft bell sounded, announcing its arrival. The door slid open. She eyed it. It was now or never. She lifted her foot a little off the floor, wavered, glanced in the direction of where she had come, then stepped in. She pressed the button for the floor but there was no movement. She did it again with the same result. "What the…" then she remembered to press her ID card against a small bar on the control panel. Voilà! The door slid closed, and she ascended.

Chapter Twenty-One

"What about Jim?" Neve countered. She straightened, seemingly no longer interested in locating her cell.

"For instance," Young began, "how often would you see him? Was it mornings? Night?"

Neve wet her lips with her tongue, then held the sides of her shirt closer together. "I… haven't you talked to the two cops who were outside the apartment? I told them pretty much what I know…really." She waited for Young to respond but was met with a stone face.

"Listen." She let go of her shirt and brushed hair from her face, "I go to school, party, then crash. I'm not good on details so leave me alone."

Brandt took over. "Neve, you have backtracked on things you've said. All we're trying to do is put the pieces together of what happened before Nicole's death. We know Nicole had an affair with Jim. He already told us. Was Nicole seeing anyone else?"

She gazed at the ceiling, then at Brandt. "What do I need to do to get you guys out of here? I'm hungover, tired, and hungry. Jesus. I don't know about Nicole's love life. She could have pulled a train. Shit. I didn't keep track of who goes in or out of her apartment. Now leave me alone."

Brandt wouldn't let go. "Did Nicole mention others?"

Neve ran her hand over her face. "Christ, she…she may have. I don't know. You know, girl shit, hi and bye, who did you fuck today. We didn't have long talks. It was nothing like that."

"You knew she was seeing Jim, right?"

She shook her head. "Yeah…I guess." She sighed and glanced in the direction of the bedroom.

"Why are you looking there?" Young followed Neve's gaze. "You have company?"

"Hell no." Neve pouted. She made a clicking sound using her tongue to roll over the roof of her mouth. "Damn. Is that a crime I looked over there? I was thinking of what I wanted to wear once you're outta here." She took a half step, stopped, then plopped back on the couch. "I'll make you drool just like Sharon Stone in… What was…*Basic*…"

"*Instinct*," Brandt answered. "Great movie but I'm not Michael Douglas."

Neve caught Young looking at Brandt. "Bet you'd like to be." She dangled her legs over the couch's edge.

"Knock it off," Brandt said. "Has Jim contacted you since Nicole's death?"

"Nope."She shook her head so that her hair flopped over her face.

"What are you doing?" Brandt stared.

"Shaking my head pretending to be a helicopter." She made the sound of a whining motor.

"Cut it out." Brandt raised his voice.

Neve got louder and mimicked its movements by slowly rising straight up from the couch.

"Where the hell are you going?"

"This is the captain our destination is the shower and will be arriving in a second or two. Have a nice flight."

"Neve, come back here." Young reached for Neve's shoulder, but she ducked aside.

"Bye, y'all. Let yourselves out. I'm about to land." She turned the faucet for the shower on. She stopped with the helicopter noise and peered over her shoulder. The two dicks were at the doorway. She slowly slid her shirt off her shoulders, down her back, and stopped at her waist. "Show's over, detectives." She let the shirt drop from her body and hopped into the shower.

"Next time you may not be so lucky, Neve. We'll be back." Young nudged Brandt away.

Neve left the shower door open and listened for the cops' retreating footsteps. She strained to hear the opening and closing of her apartment door. When she heard the click, she closed the shower and luxuriated under the running water. The tension and weariness seemed to slide off. For the first time since she woke, she felt good. No more being down. It was a new day and what had happened, happened. It was all in the past, and for her, the past lasted until her next high or experience. She turned the water off and grabbed a towel. She had one leg raised resting on her makeup chair toweling herself dry when the air changed. She looked up. Jim stood in the doorway wearing only his boxer shorts along with a shit-ass grin plastered on his face. The outline of his dick, unmistakable. "Jesus."

Chapter Twenty-Two

The elevator glided smoothly to the 6th floor. Before stepping out, Lori viewed the hallway in each direction. Seeing and hearing nothing, she walked out and went to the front glass door emblazoned with the company's name and logo. Her hands shook as she inserted her key and opened it. Entering, she saw the dim emergency lights pierced the gray darkness. The click of the door locked behind startled her. She stopped abruptly and looked wildly about. Satisfied it was only the door, she rubbed her arms to fight off the coldness of her fear. She took a deep breath. Hearing no other noise, she resolved she was okay and ready to open the large wood door separating the reception area from the offices. Jim's was down the hallway on the right-hand side near Nicole's corner spot.

Jim's door was closed but not locked. She slipped inside. His calendar was in view on his desk… a good place to start. She turned the pages to the beginning… January. She read notations. *Nicole meeting at 10* and after it a smiley face. Lori skimmed the daily pages. Nicole meetings seemed to be weekly until March. The notations and times changed. Meetings during business hours with Nicole were more frequent; what stopped Lori were the scribbles at the end of the day hours into the night. *N wants more of the same. L hasn't the faintest.* She turned the pages to a few weeks before Nicole's death. *Can't believe N had menage. There was N and…* Lori studied the next letter. She looked away then came back. Did he write N2? Who the hell was N2? She continued on. *N mentioned L. Would like to meet. What a session that would be.*

"L"? It certainly wasn't her. She hadn't had a ménage à trois. Her stomach rumbled and she broke out in a cold sweat. The pig. How could Jim…? She looked at her watch and decided to hurry. She whipped out her phone and took pictures. Was she pushing her luck to investigate Nicole's office? She opened Jim's door. Nothing had changed. The emergency lights were still on, and there were no other sounds other than her breathing. She wiped the accumulated sweat from her face, then stepped into the hallway, closing Jim's office behind. Nicole's was fifty feet away.

Nicole's door wasn't locked either. Unlike Jim's, her entire back wall was floor to ceiling glass. The view of Lake Michigan's shoreline and the Drive was spectacular. Her desk sat in the middle of the room. Off to the left was Nicole's private bathroom; to the right was a closet.

The top of her desk was sterile…no papers, folders, not even a picture. Lori's hand shook as she tried one of the drawers. It was locked as well as the next one. Damn. There had to be a key…somewhere. She bit her lip. Where? If Nicole kept it with her, then Lori's day was over and she should get the hell out. She sat in Nicole's chair and placed a hand on the desk. Her knee bumped the side. She heard a soft purr. The top drawer opened to her touch. *I'll be damned.* On top was Nicole's leather-bound appointment book. She opened to a random page and soon became engrossed. Nicole was one busy woman. Almost every hour occupied. There were meetings, social engagements, and travel. Where did she get the stamina? Did she sleep? Go to the bathroom? She also had doctor appointments, like a lot of them. She must have been a sick girl. For a moment, a bit of sympathy grabbed Lori. She closed the book. There was nothing written that had similar notations like Jim. Lori returned the volume and tried the next drawer. She lifted several sheets of paper and underneath was a key. She looked under the desk, on top, no luck. She rolled the chair back and nearly hit the credenza. *Bingo.* The key fit perfectly. Amongst files, check books, statements, was a loose-leaf notebook. As soon as she flipped several pages, her eyes widened. "Holy shit, the mother lode." Besides the dates and hours, the notes were cryptic but oh-my-God.

Had J in office then at the apartment. L & N arrived later. Fun time. Best though was X. I was ready.

Seeing too much of N. She's a good toy, but... Even J & L don't compare with X.

J tells me there's rumors the VP of the company is in trouble. Nothing like pillow talk after. Better than a cigarette.

Have to work on X. that shouldn't be...

The lights in the hallway turned on. Lori shot out of her seat holding Nicole's notebook. Reflectively she dropped it into the cadenza and closed it. She listened for footsteps that she feared were coming. *Where to go? Where to...? Bathroom?* She took a step toward it then went the other way...the closet. She heard Nicole's office door open a few seconds after Lori closed hers.

* * *

Donavan Hill caught his breath after climbing the three flights of stairs. He flicked on the office lights, then grabbed a cup of water from the dispenser in the utility room inside the office area. Age and laziness had taken their toll. It wasn't that long ago that three flights were nothing. Now, he was breathing like he'd gone ten rounds in a boxing match. He'd have to attend to that, but who was he kidding. Exercise was nearly always at the bottom of the list. Besides, if he needed his fists, he had a better solution. He was always packing. He tapped the outside of his coat and felt the holster underneath. That put him in good enough shape.

His drink did the trick. He began to walk toward Nicole's office, fingering the various office keys in his pocket. For no apparent reason he glanced down and noticed several specks of dirt on the parquet floor. He continued and came to Jim's office. For the hell of it he tried the door and was surprised it wasn't locked. He opened it and did a quick visual. Nothing seemed out of order. He probably should secure this office too. He made a mental note to return after he went through Nicole's.

Every breath Lori took sounded like an explosion. Whoever came into the office was sure to hear. She cupped a hand over her mouth. *Please God, please, please.* She stood by the closed door. The closet was pitch black. She gripped the door handle while straining for any sound. Whoever it was would go to Nicole's desk as she did. She heard a grunt. Male? Female? Then the soft roll of a drawer. Another grunt along with the rustling of paper. *Shit, the credenza, Nicole's loose-leaf...* Her index knuckle pressed against her lip. Anything to keep from shouting, crying, being found. More footsteps.

Hill saw more dirt fragments by Nicole's credenza. For the moment, he ignored the mess and used one of his keys from his pants pocket to unlock the credenza door. The wood panel door swung open. He then pulled the inside drawer forward. A loose-leaf binder rested on top of the checks, bills, and other manila files. He patted his coat once more, then scanned the room. He felt someone's presence. He let out a quiet laugh and did another quick glance. If there was somebody, it was probably someone who worked for the company. There were no secrets from him. Every square inch was wired. Cameras were everywhere. It was one of the ways the Boss maintained control. If somebody had entered, all he had to do was push a few buttons and the mystery would be revealed. Herman Jones, the downstairs guard, looked harmless, but he was paid well to report all he saw. What he missed was recorded by the security system.

Hill was familiar with Nicole's writings in her loose-leaf tell-all. He had a pretty good idea to whom the single letters referred to but not all. He was amid tracking down who "X" and "L" could be. He was pretty sure who "N" was. From the way Nicole wrote about "X" he believed it was someone high up in the company. He had advised the Boss. Even read some of the entries to him. The Boss's response was all business. He told Hill to continue to monitor Nicole's writings. Ambition as depicted in those writings and her exploits had its limits. Nicole was on her way out, although she didn't know it.

Hill took Nicole's notebook and relocked the credenza. Thank God he took it before the police or someone else. It was sloppy work on his part. He should have retrieved it the moment Nicole died.

He stood from Nicole's chair. Someone, he was sure, had been or was still in the office. He could check the bathroom and closet. On the other hand, he had the prize…Nicole's book. If he shot the intruder that would lead to unwarranted publicity and many questions. There was no need. The cameras and/or Herman would tell him. He began to walk toward Nicole's office door, but habit or curiosity got the better of him. He veered toward the bathroom brandishing his weapon. He threw the door open. The light immediately went on. He went into a crouch, his arms outstretched pointing his gun, but the room was empty. It would be ever more enjoyable to confront the intruder with the tape. He looked forward to that confrontation. He could see it unfold.

The accused would be surprised by Hill's appearance. After his introduction as to who he was, he pictured the quarry denying his accusations. Their physical actions were the tell that gave them away…dry lips, blinking eyes, their hands playing with a pen or other object. Tiny beads of sweat would appear on their brow. It was a much cleaner way of executing. The thought of delivering the coup de gr•ce brought a smile.

He reholstered his Beretta and took a breath, then glanced at his watch. He had other things to do like visiting the Boss's little brat, Neve. Whoever paid a visit to Nicole's office would get their due. Judgement Day was coming.

Lori heard the jangle of keys, then silence. *Who is there? Should I open the door?* Seconds passed as hours. The combination of fear and impatience pressed against sound judgement. *What if I open the door a crack?* She yanked the door handle down and was about to push, then remembered the overhead light would turn on. *Damn.* She let go of the handle. She had to regroup…think of something else. She couldn't stay in the closet forever. Panic. She told herself she'd be all right. She'd get out of this. She stepped back from the door and felt her pockets for her phone. Bless Apple, it had a flashlight app. All she needed to do was…Where the hell was it? If it wasn't in her coat…the purse—had to be. She sank to the floor and as noiselessly as possible felt her way through the junk. She chided herself for putting off cleaning the shit that was there. It won't happen again, she promised. She dug toward the bottom and was rewarded. She brought the cell to her lips, kissed it, then pressed the app for the light. The darkness dissipated and as she moved toward the rear, the closet became a passageway. At the end of it she saw an outline of a door. *I'll be damned.* Nicole's office connected to Jim's. How convenient. How disgusting. *Sonofabitch.*

Chapter Twenty-Three

"What do you think you're doing?" Neve finished drying her leg, then wrapped the towel around her.

"What do you mean? Baby, you were terrific with those cops. We should celebrate and what better way…" He took a half-step toward her.

"Stop right there. You need to leave."

"What? Why?" He shook his head. "Neve, I didn't kill Nicole."

"You didn't?"

"No, Goddammit. She was very much alive when I left."

Neve wrapped the towel tighter.

"I know you two were close." He laughed. "I mean…friends and shit. I had no reason or want to do Nicole harm. She helped me and I her."

Neve knew that was true from the talks she'd had with Nicole. Jim did anything Nicole asked. She and Nicole would laugh as to how whipped he was.

"Nicole and…" Jim circled the air with his arm, "you, and all of this, opened my eyes to how much more life had to give. Before I met the two of you, I was middle-aged before my time. Come on, Neve, you must have felt the same way. I get pillow talk, but I know there was more to it."

Neve blinked through newly formed tears. Jim was good with words. She did like him. He made her feel adult-like not only sexually, but he respected what she had to say. But…fucking him now after…Nicole…was wrong, or maybe slightly wrong, or was it wrong at all?

She studied him. No doubt he was ready. It wasn't only the lower part of him but his eyes. His eagerness was overcoming her reluctance.

What the hell? After the crap with the police, about Nicole, why not get some pleasure out of it. Unlike the young studs who got it on and finished in a flurry, Jim took his time. He was the antidote to fast and furious. She closed her eyes and thought of the three of them, well now he'd finally meet the fourth. He could be revved up in the right circumstances.

She decided. "Okay, Jim, get ready to party but first take a shower. While you're doing that and thinking of all the ways I'll jump your bones, I'll text our friend. She's real, you know, and invite her over."

"Wow." His mouth hung open. "Real...huh? Damn, that's fantastic!"

"I know." She allowed him to hug her. Despite the towel that clung to her she felt his arousal hard against her. "Easy boy, save it for the main event."

"I'll take a cold shower."

"Whatever works."

She heard him whistling as she went to her bedroom. She searched for something audacious to wear. Something that would rock both him and her. A lacy thong to show off her ass and a midriff shirt tied in front. Hot time in the city, she mused. She chose black for the bottoms and ivory for the top. She slipped on what there was of the clothing and checked herself in the mirror. She ruled. All she had to do now was find her phone to text their friend. She took a minute, then remembered. She'd dropped it in a bureau drawer in the dining room along with the brandy glass. She congratulated her recall and at the same time chided herself for being stupid for not remembering.

Finally, she held her cell in her hands. It was like finding a long-lost friend. Its slick sides felt s-o-o good. She saw there were several messages but first things first. The party had to start soon. The poor boy couldn't stay in the shower much longer. She curled herself onto a chair and began her text.

L time for some loving, going to fuck ourselves silly. We'll makeup for Nicole. I have a surprise for you. So, get your ass here pronto. Make an excuse to get rid of your partner. N.

She pressed "Send" and took a moment delighting in the good time that was about to happen. She shivered at the anticipation of being touched and fondled. Her breath quickened as well as her heart. The inspired prelude swept away any lingering depressing thoughts.

The pounding on the front door brought her back.

* * *

"Open up," Donavan Hill's voice was contemptuous. "You little bitch," he said to himself.

He had parked across the street from Neve's building in time to observe what he believed were two plain-clothes officers leave. He'd sat in his car for at least 15-20 minutes waiting to see if something else occurred.

Hill could never just relax. His mind was always going. He contacted Herman at the company's building and asked if he had found anyone on the camera footage. The guard's response was "no." That answer didn't sit well. He tried to hold his anger in check.

"There can't be too much tape to look through. You have the date and a two-hour window…three at most."

"It don't go like that, sir. The system ain't made to pinpoint hours. It's by days."

"What? Can't be!"

"I'm try'n to tell you. It old, Mr. Hill. I've asked to upgrade but noth'n happened. We got to wait until end of the day to get the video."

Hill choked back his response for a second or two. "Do what you have to do but get the damn video." He disconnected and threw his phone onto the passenger seat. It was hard to believe. He glanced out the car window while he fumed. Not seeing anything to make him cautious, he left for Neve's apartment.

Chapter Twenty-Four

Lori stepped closer to the connecting door in the passageway between Nicole's office closet and Jim's. It wasn't only the images of Jim and Nicole cavorting in secret that disgusted her, but the dishonesty. How could they—screw "they"—Jim continue every day and not show guilt or remorse? How could he touch her, make love to her, all the while he's banging Nicole? If he could compartmentalize like that, what else could he do? She stopped herself from inflicting more mental torment.

The larger and more immediate issue was how to get out of this situation. If she opened this connecting door, would someone be waiting? Shit. She felt like a mouse trapped between two hungry cats. What to do? Nature's call provided the impetus. Nicole's office had a bathroom and more importantly, she'd grab Nicole's tell-all loose-leaf book. She turned around and moved toward the other closet door. Her hand gripped the handle. She took a couple of deep breaths and thought of her grandmother's saying: "With luck you drive the world."

She opened the closet a touch, which turned on the light. She peered into Nicole's office, which was dark but for the glow of the emergency system. Satisfied no one else was there, she opened the door wider. She took a step into the office closing the door behind her. Her bladder made the choice of what needed to be done first. She made her way to the bathroom. As she sat on the padded cushy toilet seat, two things crossed her mind. Nicole was lucky and rich. Lori's grandmother's saying popped into her mind again. She got the quote wrong. It wasn't luck but money that drove the world. Neither of which she had. One thing for sure, though, she felt much better after the bathroom break. She washed her hands and went to dry them. The hot air contraption would make too much noise. Where was the towel dispenser? She glanced around the room, looking. A recessed, small, faded bluish light above the wash basin caught her eye. She stared at it and had the silly notion that it could be a camera. Why the hell would there be a recording device in a bathroom? She splashed water on her face and looked up again. The thing seemed to blink. This was too crazy. She had to get out of there.

She went to Nicole's desk to retrieve the key for the credenza. Her hand shook a little as she inserted and turned it, then pulled the drawer open… so far so good. She was certain she left Nicole's tell-all on top of the files and other junk.

It wasn't there.

"Damn, damn, damn." The frustration of the day welled up and she was near tears. She plopped herself on Nicole's chair and rubbed her face to remain calm. Now what? She glanced at the open credenza. Could Nicole's book have fallen toward the back? She was about to search but knew that wasn't the case. The binder was too thick. The reality of someone having taken it slapped her in the face.

She turned from the credenza to the mostly barren desk and fixated on the opposite wall, staring at the fleur-de-lis wallpaper design. Was Jim here and grabbed it? Or was it someone else who didn't want those details uncovered? Nicole's little exposé of who, what, and where was too hot to remain in the credenza. Christ. She rubbed her hands together. If it wasn't Jim, was it someone in the company? Those thoughts danced in her head as she followed the wallpaper design to the ceiling border. She blinked. There it was again. A fuck'n recessed faded blue light twinkled like a star saying, "good evening." Her stomach did a loop and she shuddered. The goddamn place was bugged. Cameras. Oh shit. She felt her face get hot. For a moment she sat in shock. All of the ramifications of being videoed went through her head. When she was able to breathe, a bizarre thing happened. A picture of Jim with his pants down flashed. She let out a laugh. Oh, Jimbo, you fool, you didn't know who you were playing with. Nicole was the appetizer and the rest you never saw.

Chapter Twenty-Five

Young followed Brandt down the stairs from Neve's apartment.

She waited until they were out of the building and near their car before exploding. "That skank. We should have hauled her ass and thrown it into a goddamn cell, so she'd learn what life was really about."

"Don't take it so hard. Neve gave us a hint that Nicole may have had other lovers. She also confirmed our prime suspect had an ongoing affair with Nicole. All in all, not a total waste." He looked over at his partner. "You still look pissed. You want me to drive."

Young shrugged. "Sure."

Brandt went to the driver's side and used his fob to unlock the car.

Young grabbed the outside door handle, got in, then slammed her side shut.

"Hey partner, cool down. Think of it as theater...a whodunnit. The script has already been written, we just need to find the players. With luck and time, we'll find them."

"The bitch has no shame. Why aren't you pissed, Brandt? Parading around like that, getting naked and throwing us out. Jesus, what happened to respect, decency?"

"Well, Charlie," he turned to her. "Can I call you that?"

The use of that name caught her by surprise. "How did...?"

Brandt smiled. "There are few secrets in the department. We're cops. We snoop. We gossip. We get the four-one-one."

"Okay, Columbo, but only between us. *Capiche?*"

Brandt nodded. "Got it. It's a hanged world. I sound like an old fart, but that's the truth. It's not only Neve; disrespect for us, for rules, is everywhere. Neve is a privileged bitch whose parents gave her anything and everything...nothing new there. Why worry about us when daddy has taken care of every bump in her life. The spoiled rich kid syndrome has always been; what changed are the attitudes of the rest of society. It reminds me of a juvenile case I had a while back. The little bitch offed a fellow student for posting some garbage on the internet. What was her name…? Jesus, getting old is a bitch. I think it was Ann…something like that. Her family thought she was an angel. If I remember right, she looked like one, too."

Young sighed. "You got that right. Neve's parents probably sent her to the best schools and bought her a car at sixteen."

"What are you talking?" Brandt grinned. "She had a Beamer with all the trimmings. Nothing too good for daddy's little girl."

Young glanced at Brandt. "You're on target …the little shit. I didn't get a car until I was out of college and it sure wasn't new."

Brandt tapped his hand on the wheel. "Console yourself, Charlie, most of us don't have Neve's life. If you think about it, probably wouldn't want it. It's good to be grounded. To have a grasp of right and wrong and be able to think beyond the immediate. Hell, I'm preaching. I'll shut up."

Young nodded but only half-listened. She had felt her phone vibrate, notifying her of an incoming message, while Brandt jabbered. She ignored the urge to read it, stayed quiet, and watched the grit of the city pass by.

"Hey, Charlie, you there? Was it something I said?"

"What? No, sorry. I can't get Neve out of my mind…such a little brat. Jesus."

Brandt made a turn, and their police station came into view. "I thought when we get back, we would track down those doctors Nicole used."

"Good idea." Young shifted in her seat. "Can you drop me at my car?"

"What? Why?"

"I'm going back there. I have a hunch."

"What hunch?"

"Hard to explain, but I think someone was there with Neve."

"Okay, but…"

"Trust me, Brandt, trust me."

"Suit yourself. Just don't do anything stupid." He pulled up alongside her vehicle.

Young got out and jumped into her car. She roared out of the parking lot and raced down Fullerton until she was several blocks away. She checked her mirrors to make sure Brandt or someone else hadn't followed, then reached into her pocket for her phone. Her eyes widened and she took quick, short breaths as she read the message. A few seconds later she responded, "On my way," and added a smiley face emoji.

* * *

Hill knocked repeatedly on Neve's door. The little bitch was wasting his time. He had more important things to do than checking on her welfare. Then again, what the hell were those cops doing at the building? What did the little slut say to them? He looked at his watch. Jesus, late afternoon, what was taking so long to answer? "Neve, open the door."

He thought he heard voices and shuffling of feet. He pressed his hand on the doorknob. It opened a crack and jerked to a stop.

"Who's there?"

"Damn it, Neve, take the chain off and let me in. It's Donavan Hill."

"What do you want? I didn't text you."

"Stop playing games. Either open the door or I'll bust it."

He heard the chain slide off. He didn't wait and pushed the door open. Neve stood a foot away, her arms folded against her chest.

He stepped in and saw her dressed in only a thong and midriff shirt. "Getting ready to entertain?" He smirked. "I mean fuck." He stepped around her. "Your butt is perfect." He gave it a slap.

"Ouch." She rubbed her ass.

"Who's the lucky guy or maybe gal?" He peered into the living room but didn't see anyone. "Come on, Neve, where's the lucky john or jane?"

"Get out. Why are you here?"

He circled her again like a meat inspector and let out a low whistle. "I know you and the late whore upstairs, Nicole, fucked your brains out. According to her you were quite willing to spread your legs for anyone. Her little tell-all makes for compelling reading."

"Shut up. I don't know what you're talking about. Nicole didn't write anything. You're making it up. You liar. Daddy should have fired you long ago." She inched away from him, edging herself out of the hallway.

He grabbed her around her neck and forced her backward into a wall. "Maybe I should get you all warmed up, but first," his face was close to hers, "what did you tell the cops?"

"Cops? Let go, you bastard."

"Tell me, you little shit." While his hand was on her neck, he undid her midriff shirt. "I always appreciated your tits."

"You'll never get to have them."

He applied more pressure.

"I can't... let...go. You're...hurting..."

"That's the point. Now what..."

He was interrupted by the ringing of his phone. He slid his hand off her neck to answer but stayed close enough to block her escape.

"What's that, Herman?" He glanced at Neve. She stayed frozen, her eyes wide.

"The system is down at the building. How's that..." Hill took a step back. "I'll be there in twenty minutes. Don't call the police."

He ended the conversation and pointed his index finger at Neve. "We'll continue our little chat and get-together later. As far as your daddy is concerned, I know you'll keep your mouth shut. You wouldn't want me to tell him what I learned from your late friend." He backed away from her. "If you did talk to the cops, you're smart enough to have said little. Isn't that right?"

Neve rubbed her neck slowly. "Yeah," she said staring at the floor. "Didn't say a thing."

Hill stuck his hand under her chin. "I like to look at a face when they or I talk."

She raised her head with his help.

"Good. Very good. I won't keep you from your party." He looked past her again for signs of someone else there. Not seeing anything or anyone, he turned toward the front door but stopped. She hadn't moved from her place near the wall.

"It better not be Jim you're about to entertain. Of course, he'd be dumber than shit to be here with you, but men don't always think with their heads. At least not the one between their shoulders. You call me if he shows. Understood?"

She didn't move.

"Do you…" He took a step towards her.

"Yeah, I got you," her voice subdued.

If he had the power to use his eyes and set her on fire, he would have. The effect of his stare, though, accomplished what he wanted. It left her shaking.

Chapter Twenty-Six

Lori kept an eye on the faded blue light in the ceiling tile. Somewhere on the other end someone probably was watching her.

Did Nicole know? Did she plant them there herself? If she didn't... Lori drummed her fingers on Nicole's desk. Why would Nicole want to be recorded while doing Jim and whoever else? She wouldn't. So, what did Nicole do?

Lori glanced around Nicole's office. Nothing obvious popped out. Time was ticking away, and she'd better come up with a solution, soon. Hell, Google it, why not? She whipped out her phone and put in several key phrases. An answer scrolled across her screen. A laser pen would dismantle the camera. Bless that little search engine. Now where would she find such a thing? She pressed the button on the side of Nicole's desk and unlocked the drawers. She rifled through the first one, the second, then the middle.

Paperclips, pencils, pens, were lined up in their plastic organizer. Nicole must have been a neat freak. She went through the pens again but none of them appeared to be a laser. Shit. She checked her watch. She could feel her minutes running out. If anyone looked at the video... God help me. She observed the plastic tray. What if...? She placed her hands around the sides and lifted. Damn, there it was, underneath. *You sneaky girl, Nicole but thank you.*

She had to check Google again for exactly what needed to be done. Following the instructions, she left Nicole's chair and went where she'd seen the dull light at the far end of the office ceiling. She turned on the laser and pointed. She heard a pop and then smelled the odor from an electrical fire. "Holy crap." She ran to

Nicole's bathroom and did the same thing with the same results. It was time to go. Really go.

She didn't remember if she shut Nicole's office door or the door leading to the waiting area. The only thought was to get out. When she reached the elevators, she pushed the button for one, then realized how stupid. There had to be stairs. *Somewhere are goddamn stairs.* She glanced down the hall one way, then the other. At the far corner was the sign for it. *Thank God.* Hurry. She raced to that end and tried the door. It didn't move. A soft bell announced an elevator's arrival. She glared back toward it with her hand gripping the handle of the blocking door. In a second or two the elevator would open. She pulled the handle towards her then pushed. The door opened. She slipped through and gently closed it.

Jogging down six flights of stairs would be her exercise for the day. Her leg muscles would remind her of their misuse later. Upon reaching the lobby, she caught her breath. If her memory was correct, the exit was a distance behind the security desk. Before she opened the exit door, she said a silent prayer for the guard to be on the 6th floor or watching his small TV engrossed in the football game. Fortune needed to be smiling upon her, whatever her grandmother's saying.

* * *

"It was the darndest thing, Mr. Hill. I watched the switches that tell me the cameras are work'n, then suddenly the whole bank go dark. Looky here."

Hill glanced at the board Herman pointed to and grunted.

"Then, I sees over here an elevator was called to the sixth floor." Herman pointed to another row of switch lights. "I figure something's up, so I hop on. When I gets there, there's no one. Whoever it be, I think is slick, so I draw my weapon. Mr. Hill, honestly, I've never done that before. But I have a job to do. I goes in and there's Miss Nicole's office door wide open. Now I'm really worried. I head in but damn not a soul there. I look up and the cameras blown to hell. Excuse me, Mr. Hill, I mean destroyed. Now why a person do that is beyond me. They could hit the toggle below the light switch. It shut the whole thing off."

Hill half-listened to the guard while adding and subtracting suspects who came to mind. "Okay, Herman." Hill cleared his throat. "Can any of the video be salvaged?"

"I… let me put it this way, highly unlikely. I don't know the technical jazz but once the circuit go, so do everything else."

"I see. Call the company that installed the system to make sure."

"Yes sir."

"Herman, do you remember anyone coming in?"

Herman scratched his head. "I got here a little after eleven, you know. The place ain't busy on a Sunday. I had my TV on to pass the time. Didn't see noth'n to give me pause. I knew you were in the building and maybe a few others."

"How many…others? Male? Female? What floor did they go?"

"Aw Mr. Hill, I…I…don't really know. I remember a fella came in, I think he work on Four, and a woman a little later."

"About what time did this woman come in?"

Herman couldn't escape Hill's stare. He wiped his face. "Let's see. The Bears were down

by a field goal and the Packers were about to score another time. Must have been in the first…no… no later than second quarter."

"Do you remember what floor?"

"Floor? Hmm… No sir, I honestly don't. She wasn't someone who regularly be here on a Sunday…that for sure."

"Did she use her ID to get past the machines?"

Small beads of sweat formed on the sides of Herman's hairline. "I wish I could tell you she did, but on Sundays they're disabled. She showed it, and I waved her through."

Hill moved within a foot or two from the guard. "Think carefully, Herman. Do you remember the name on the ID or the company?"

"Name?" Herman's face paled. "I…I… Mr. Hill…she sort of flashed it, you know, real fast like…and I…"

"Let her through."

Herman nodded.

Hill stepped back. He knew Herman had nothing more to add. "If something comes to mind, Herman, ring me."

"Yes sir, I do that."

Hill started to leave but stopped. "Did you see her leave the building?"

Herman looked up towards the ceiling. "Nah, can't say I did."

"What about the cameras in the stairwell?"

Chapter Twenty-Seven

eve stayed next to the hallway wall after Hill left. His threat was clear. Her free-ride world was in the hands of one Donavan Hill. She rubbed her neck, then slumped to the floor where she sat cross-legged. The last few days, the last few minutes, her life—boiled over and she sobbed.

"Who the hell was that?"

Neve looked up. Jim came from the bedroom with only a towel around his middle. Tears streaked down her face. "Yours… and….my…worst…. nightmare," she sniffed.

"Huh? A cop?"

She shook her head. "No".

"Tell me." He stooped. "What's wrong with you? Are you crying? What happened to your neck. A hickey?"

"Shut up." She looked at him through tear-bleary eyes. "You…you have…to…leave." She wiped her nose with her arm.

He held out his hand. "Let me help you up." She didn't move. "Unless your little brain is cooking up some kind of kinky sex."

"Fuckoff. I'll get up on my own." She knocked his hand away and stood.

"I… What just happened? Neve, talk to me. Whatever it is, we can… Jesus. What happened to the party girl and all that fun? The cops are under control. What can be so bad? Come on…there's a lot of good times waiting…" His focus went to her partially exposed breasts.

She gave him a long stare, then looked down at her chest and tied her shirt. She shook her head in disbelief. "I've never been accused of having smarts, but you must really be dumb. You don't know who that man was?"

Jim's smile disappeared. He shrugged and raised his arms. "No, I honestly don't. Should I?"

"You poor naïve fool. That's Donavan Hill…Daddy's *consigliere* and hatchet man rolled into one. He's the man who takes care of all of Daddy's problems." She brushed hair out of her eyes. "Can you get me Kleenex, for God's sake?"

"Sure…sure." He came back from the bathroom with several tissues.

Neve blew her nose, then balled the used ones up.

"Hey, Neve." His hands touched his hips. "We can start the party here. I got something I know you crave."

"Don't you dare. Will you get your filthy mind off that. Let me paint you a picture." She mimed reading a book. She could tell he didn't follow. "You don't get it, do you? He's got Nicole's diary."

"Book? You were reading a book. What game are we playing?"

Neve glared at him. "Christ, Jim, Nicole kept track of who she fucked and when. She named names. I'm in it and so are you. You're a problem and I'm a great disappointment."

"Me? What…"

His face paled as recognition slowly washed over him.

"Holy shit, now…" He placed his index finger to the side of his head and cocked his thumb. "Holy shit, now it makes sense."

"What does?"

"The night I was released from the police station."

"Yeah?"

"Something happened."

"Like what?"

"Not important, but it's clear." He reached out for Neve's shoulders. "I had a feeling that someone's hand was moving pieces. Now I know. Your daddy or Hill wants to pin what happened to Nicole on me. I'm going to put a stop to that."

"You're going to…and how will you do that?"

"Confront him and your dad."

She brushed his hands away. "You're stupider than me. Shit."Tears of anger and exasperation trickled down her face. "You…you…have…no…idea…who…you're…messing   with."

She took deep breaths, frustrated by his lack of comprehension. "You have to leave. They will crush you as well as me. Get your fuck'n clothes and get the hell away."

His face lost all color. "I've no place to go. Lori threw me out."

She took a small step away from him and toward the living room. "That's your problem. There are hotels. I'll give you a few hundred. Pay me back whenever."

"You really want me to leave?" His towel slipped and he grabbed it before it fell.

She stared. Earlier before Hill, she had pictured Jim's body, strong and appealing, a good time to be had. Now with only a bath sheet wrapped around him, he looked pathetic, like a dog who had been kicked. "Yeah. Get the... Hill will be coming back here, and..."

"Neve, baby, this doesn't have to end," he argued. "We can get help."

"How stupid are you? Look around. Do you think I can afford this?"

"But your..." He stopped. "Oooh! Hill is blackmailing you, too?"

She took a deep breath. "Everyone has a price, Jim, and I'll pay it if I have to."

"Whattabout the other player in your little group that I was going to meet. Was she named also?"

His question brought a quick smile to her. "You have...Oh shit, I forgot."She marched over to the couch, grabbed her phone, thought for a minute, then sent a text.

* * *

Charlie circled around Neve's neighborhood searching for a parking space. Even cops had to park legally on occasion. This arrangement had blossomed into something quite different from what had originally been proposed. She was to keep an eye on Neve, a sort-of private eye thing on her off hours.

Charlie's ex-boyfriend, the one she threw out four months prior had asked if she was interested in making extra cash. An acquaintance of his knew a wealthy guy in Atlanta whose daughter would be attending college in Chicago. The dad thought a female would be better suited. Charlie agreed. She was paid a semester in advance.

Charlie found a space but kept the motor running. The city paid for the gas. She flicked the radio to a jazz station. She wanted to look real good before knocking on Neve's door. Might as well play something to get the blood going even though it was going all ready. It would only take a few more minutes.

Thinking back, she should have asked more questions, certainly after her ex gave her a bundle of Franklins as payment. He explained it was how corporate rich folks do things. In his words, "No big deal." She was sure her ex kept a portion as a "finder's fee." There was enough for her not to make a difference.

Charlie was aware that taking cash meant the whole arrangement was "under the table." She rationalized, though, it wasn't a bribe. She handled the assignment straight and reported what she saw.

There were a few strings that went along with the gig. Obviously, Neve must not know, and Charlie was to provide weekly reports addressed to his company in Chicago in care of Nicole McMaster.

Charlie turned the car's rear view mirror towards her as she reached into her purse for a brush.

It was easy work. On her off days, Charlie waited outside Neve's apartment and observed. Neve attended class on a sometime basis. Her usual routine consisted of late mornings, Starbucks, an occasional class or two, Starbucks, and partying. Despite the lackadaisical approach, Neve's schoolwork didn't suffer much—an occasional B in a crowd of C's. If Neve spotted her, she never let on. Seemed like she didn't care.

The job ended when Charlie tossed her ex out. She had one more report due and, true to giving value for the money, decided to deliver it in person.

Charlie dipped into her purse for lipstick. Neve liked red; so did Nicole. "Ruby red," Nicole ordered, "the color of a seductress." That was Nicole. Charlie leaned into the car mirror and applied the lipstick carefully.

Jesus, the first time she met Nicole was at Nicole's office. They discussed Neve's boyfriends, their background checks, and her school. Nicole asked Charlie to stay on the job and she'd pay. That should have been a tipoff, at least a yellow light, but Charlie didn't think twice. The money was good and if this crazy broad wanted to pay, so be it. Their meetings became more frequent, not only at Nicole's office but for coffee or lunch.

Nicole did her thing, but Charlie didn't catch-on. The coup de grâce happened three weeks later. She met not only Nicole, but also Neve at Nicole's apartment. Charlie was surprised at first, awkward, but after a few drinks and smokes, everything and everyone warmed up. Neve didn't miss a beat when Charlie confessed she had been following her at school for her dad. Neve explained that's what he always did.

Many more conversations and get-togethers followed. When Charlie had time off, she'd find herself with Neve and Nicole. Many a night was spent at Nicole's. *What a goddamn beautiful place.* Their talks augmented by much wine, weed, and sometimes stunning white powder, led to an outpouring of feelings and warmth. Nicole sucked all that up and used it. She reeled Charlie in like a fish. Any resistance gave way to the pleasures derived. A few times Neve seemed put off by it, like Charlie had taken her place. She'd pout, threaten she had a headache, but then Nicole would lure her back. Charlie didn't believe anyone missed a man on those occasions.

Charlie did a final check of her face and hair. Everything was in place. If she'd known this party was going to happen, she would have worn the new thong she bought the other day. Her clothes would have to do. Besides, if all went well, she wouldn't be in them for long.

She was aware of Jim from Nicole who let slip Neve partied with them at times. Neve would intimate Nicole had others. It was like an old *Mad Magazine* episode of *Spy vs. Spy*. Nicole and Neve knew certain secrets of the other and used Charlie to find out more.

Nicole's death naturally complicated everything. Jesus, Charlie knew the players. Nicole—God, Nicole. Was her death due to excess or someone? Charlie couldn't, no, make that wouldn't, tell Brandt of her involvement. There'd be too many questions. Not only about the sex, Christ, the whole department would be snickering, but the money and God the coke never disclosed. All that could cost her career. Hell, she'd be lucky to get a job flipping burgers or worse—possible jail. She caught her breath. Why let her imagination ruin the good time around the corner.

Neve was the only one who knew and so far, hadn't sold her out. Neve did a damn good job of playing the bitch while she and Brandt were in her apartment.

All of these rambling thoughts came to a screeching halt with the text Charlie received. She had her fob in her hand and was about to leave when she read Neve's message:

"Sorry. Had to leave. Don't come by. Party crashed. Not home."

Damn. Images of a naked agile Neve and Jim flashed through her head. She was hot with no place to go. What the hell happened?

Chapter Twenty-Eight

Lori made it out the side exit of the building without setting off alarms. She thanked God for that. She pulled her coat collar up to cover as much of her face as possible for two blocks. Exhausted, she stuck her hand out for a cab—the expense be damned. It didn't take long before a taxi stopped. Unlike the rainbow one from the night before, this cab was yellow. The driver only asked, "Where to," and left her alone with her thoughts. She closed her eyes, her mind running off.

What began as "let's see what Jim was up to" became more than she ever imagined. Hidden cameras, videos, a tell-all, holy shit, she found herself in a league she never played in or ever wanted to. This was CIA, FBI crap she read in the papers or watched on the news. She didn't know from affairs, office sex, or spying. Hell, she majored in American Literature. Call it a sheltered life…humdrum…went to work, shared a home, a bed, had friends. The complaints were everyday gripes… nothing like this. She went to sleep one evening and woke up thrust into becoming a Nancy Drew character. She never liked those books, anyway.

She opened her eyes and saw they were heading east towards DuSable Outer Drive instead of the Kennedy expressway. She asked why and he replied, "Bears Game, too much traffic." She didn't mind. The view of the lake on the right and beautiful buildings on the left gave her a small lift from her troubles. There was a bit of magic taking the Drive. The road hugged Lake Michigan's shoreline and the sun bounced off many of the glass buildings on the other side. It was postcard perfect. A glimpse of what the city could be, but in reality, never was.

She took her phone from her purse. She quickly glanced at the number of messages and for the moment ignored them. Instead, she went to the photos of Jim's calendar and reread the entries. Jim's use of initials"N2" and "L" plagued her for the rest of the trip. They obviously represented people, but who? Was "N2" another person named Nicole? Mentally, she ran through a list of people she knew from work, or acquaintances that could possibly be involved. It was a futile endeavor, and she gave up with a sigh.

The cab reached her house before she checked her messages. She paid the driver forty dollars and considered it a bargain. He left with a wave. She went to her front door and checked over her shoulder for a rainbow-colored vehicle parked on the street. Not seeing one, she dug out her key and opened the door. The smell of tobacco hit her as she walked in. "Jim? What are you doing? Is that you?"

* * *

Herman hit a switch for the video of the stairwell. Hill stood behind him to view the monitor.

"These cameras record, don't they?" Hill had an edge in his voice.

Herman, with his eyes fixed on the view of the stairs, slowly shook his head. "No, sir, I…I…Dese cameras are in real time. If someone was in the stairwell right now, we'd see'em, but recording…nah, unless I press this button over here." He pointed.

Hill looked away and fought to contain himself. "I can't believe it."

"Wait a minute…There's a shadow. Someone just opened the side door."

Hill grabbed Herman's shoulder and pushed him out of the way. "Where? Show me?"

"There. Too late. Whoever that was is out the door."

Hill stumbled over Herman's foot as he went toward that exit. Herman stuck his arm out to help Hill regain his balance. Hill slapped it away and straightened. "Get out of my way, damn it," and shoved Herman into his swivel chair. He sprinted the distance of a half of football field to the area seen on the screen. He pulled the door open and stepped outside. He saw several people walking at a normal pace. Before he turned in the opposite direction, something caught his eye. About a block or so ahead, he spotted someone who held their coat collar up darting between several people. It was cold but not wintry. He thought it could be a woman by her figure. He watched until he lost sight. To make sure he didn't miss anything he turned the other way but there was nothing to see out of the ordinary. The cold started to seep through his clothes. He pushed on the same door he had exited…Locked. He had to go to the front. He muttered to himself. His anger rose—the bitch was getting away. The frustration of the day pounded through his head. Someone had been snooping in his building. Damn it. What the hell would he tell his boss, or should he? All because of that whore Nicole. She was the cause of all this commotion, her and the little sniveling good-for-nothing Neve. Well, she was good for something and maybe he'd find out. He concentrated on those thoughts as he went through the revolving door and kept walking.

"See anything, Mr. Hill?"

Hill looked up. "What?" He saw Herman standing by the entrance. "What was that?" He repeated.

Herman's face showed concern as well as fear. *Well, the sonofabitch should be scared.* He was tempted to fire him on the spot but restrained himself. "Too late. Whoever it was got at least a block head start. I'm pretty sure it was a she. Most likely the same woman you saw earlier this afternoon."

Herman lowered his head. "Sorry, sir…I…"

Hill waved his hand. "Never mind. Keep an eye as to who leaves the building and if it's the same bitch you saw earlier, detain her, then call. Anything you don't understand?"

"No sir, I get it."

Hill nodded. "I'm going upstairs to get my things."

Herman walked Hill to the elevator and pressed the button for him. The ride to the third floor was swift. Hill walked briskly to his office and grabbed his coat from a chair. He picked up the envelope laying on his desk that had photos of Jim with the hired bimbo, as well as Nicole's loose-leaf and dropped the items into his briefcase. The image of the woman with her collar up flashed through his mind. Shit. He grabbed his cell phone and called his man, Skinny. After the third ring, a male voice answered.

"Skinny, this is Mr. Hill. I want you to do something for me."

Chapter Twenty-Nine

Neve sat on her couch with a view of Jim in her bedroom. He didn't bother to close the door as he dropped the towel to get dressed. He certainly had a nice body, good abs, nice ass, and stuff. She curled her feet under her. She watched his show that she was certain was for her benefit. When he finished dressing, he slung his coat over his shoulder and stood in the doorway.

"Well? Is this it?"

She got up and went by him. He probably expected her to do something—touch him, kiss him—but she didn't. Ignoring him, she walked to her closet. She knew what his eyes focused on. Her back was to him as she threw on a pair of sweatpants over her thong. She could almost hear him salivate. She reached for a hoodie and wore it over her shirt.

"Come on, Neve…you…"

"Stop whining. We can't be together. Don't even try. Let's go." She led him from the bedroom through the living room to the kitchen. "Use the backstairs. I don't know if Hill is still out there." She unlocked the back door and stood to the side as he stepped by. She closed it as soon as he left. Her hand rested on the doorknob as she listened to his footsteps fade down the stairs. Another person out of her life. She had a history of people trudging down the stairs on her. At least this problem was solved—for the moment. If Hill comes… Neve moved from the door and returned to the couch. She knew with every fiber of her body It wasn't a matter of *if* Hill comes but *when.* At least Jim was gone.

She took a deep breath and took in her apartment. She glanced at the picture hanging over the fireplace. It was one her mother had painted years ago. The memory of her mother laboring over her easel, a thin paintbrush in her hand, was so vivid. She felt her mother's kiss on top of her head and heard her voice. God. She shuddered and wrapped her arms around herself for warmth.

"You are such a pretty girl, I'm so sorry. I have to leave. Daddy wouldn't like it if Mommy was still in the house."

Neve watched as her mother stepped onto the porch. A cab pulled up and the driver ran up the 5 steps to help her take her suitcases. She got into the back seat of the car. Her mom didn't wave goodbye.

She was her daddy's consolation prize in the divorce. It wasn't that he really wanted her. Daddy always reminded her everything was a contest with winners and losers. There was no coming in second. Mom lost the custody battle. She died soon after.

Neve moved to another spot on the couch. She inherited the ability to manipulate from her daddy. Guilt was a great ploy for an eleven-year-old to use and use it she did. Daddy rarely said no. A car was hers at sixteen and not just any old car—brand-spank'n new red convertible. Curfews, if there was one, were never enforced. She knew how to get what she wanted. Daddy viewed her as an expensive pet. He didn't devote much time to her, and as long as she behaved in a manner that sucked up to his ego and position, she'd get what she wanted. It was very much benign neglect.

However, as she got older, she got the sense her game was beginning to wear thin. Daddy was getting tired of her excuses and especially the money she was costing. She dropped out of several schools. He warned that Chicago was her last stop at college. Besides, she was on the cusp of adulthood. If she screwed up, she'd be on her own. Was that a warning or a threat? She took it less seriously, after Nicole moved in.

Neve stood. Her apartment was so quiet. She began to pace. Nicole. What a crazy ass bitch. She was more daring than Neve ever thought to be. Nicole told her she was aware of the risk of getting involved with Jim. She took the chance and got her management position anyway.

Nicole invited Neve into her life…much of her life. Or maybe just the part Nicole wanted Neve to see.

Neve stopped her wandering and bit her thumbnail. Jesus, Nicole manipulated her just as she did her daddy. She got Neve to do things she never imagined. There was the sex…God, there was the sex. First the thrill of the ménage à trois with Jim. That was something she had thought about but was never brave enough to do. Nicole had no problem helping her cross that bridge.

It was the other thing, of being intimate with another woman, that brought a new dimension into Neve's life. Nicole made her feel…Christ… wanted, special, God…loved? She was put off when Charlie joined, then went along with it. Hell, Neve didn't want to lose…lose what? Nicole?

Nicole was gone now. Neve no longer had to worry about intimacy with Nicole—dead was dead. No more bedtime romps or spooning afterwards. Nicole gently kissing the top of her head—like her mother used to do. Dead.

Neve rubbed her face with her hands. *Snap out of it.* She reached for her cell phone and thought of calling her daddy but slowly put it down. In a contest between her or his business, she'd lose and lose big. She was very aware of how much Hill was part of Daddy's interworkings. Hill knew where many of Daddy's skeletons were because he put them there. Damn it to hell.

She really should get something to eat. Leave the apartment and get some air. She went for her purse but stopped. No, Hill was coming back. The look in his eyes told her all she needed to know. Should she act hard to get or seduce him and wear something that teased his prick—it wouldn't take much. Let him think he's got her in his clutches. *Shit, what he sees doesn't mean he has. We're both wanting the ear of the same audience…Daddy.*

She was eleven years old again and damn sure she knew what to do.

Chapter Thirty

Skinny drove his old Malibu to the address Mr. Hill gave. It sure was pretty. There were big old trees along the parkway overlooking large homes. It was a part of Chicago he knew existed but had never been. Folks who didn't quite have enough for Lincolnwood settled here. It was good thinking. He drove past the target and parked five doors down. No sense giving neighbors something to talk about. He wore a jacket that read "Jones Locksmith–Anytime" on the back.

Skinny had been in the business long enough to have disguises for all occasions. In addition, he carried a black bag with his tools of the trade—sort-of-to-speak. He was as handy with a screwdriver as he was a camera. Photos were easier and usually there was a woman involved, or the use of one like Whirley. God darn, what a time he'd have with her; choice, that's what she was—choice.

He walked up the target's driveway. When he got to the door, he dipped into his bag for the right tool, looked over his shoulder, then inserted it into the opening and flipped the lock. Easy, if you knew what you were doing. There was no lock Skinny couldn't open—at least so far. He was a professional. Even in his field, he took continuous education seriously. You're only as good as your last job.

He had 15 seconds to shut off the alarm after he opened the door. He studied the keyboard, smiled, reached into his bag again, and with another instrument, read the code that disabled the siren…nothing to it. According to Mr. Hill, he was pretty sure no one was home, but to make sure, he called out. There was no answer. He stepped from the hallway to the sunken living room. To his right was the bar. Why not? He took a glass and poured from an already opened bottle of bourbon. It did go down smooth.

Ain't noth'n like rich people's booze. They know the good stuff. When he finished, he left the glass in the bar's sink.

His instructions were to search the place for anything related to Jim and Nicole. More importantly, Jim and the woman he lived with should know someone had been there. Skinny took a moment to plan. He dug a cigar out of his pocket. What's better after a drink than a smoke? He lit up. Yes sir, he had himself a sweet job. He considered himself lucky to have it.

He worked quickly, going through drawers in the kitchen, then in the master bedroom and study. There was not much to find. He returned to the front part of the house when he heard the motor of a car pull up the driveway. He went to the front door and heard a female voice say, "Thank you."

Time to go. He went quickly down the hallway to the kitchen and left through the back as he heard the front door open.

* * *

Lori stood still in the alcove near the entry door after calling Jim's name. She glanced at the front part of her house. The sunken living room area appeared undisturbed. The furnace kicked in and she jumped at the sound. Her heart pounded. Seconds ticked by before she felt confident enough to move from her spot. She walked as quietly as she could past the living room where the smell of tobacco was heavy through the hallway to the kitchen.

The rear door was ajar.

She took a breath and went to the door and threw it open. Nothing. She slammed it shut and double-locked it. She chastised herself for being reckless and stupid. *What if someone had been out there? Then what?* She was breathing so rapidly that she put her hand over her heart to somehow slow it down.

Oh shit, was there someone upstairs in the bedrooms? She looked wildly around but saw and heard no one. Should she call the police? Run—get a neighbor?

What the hell had she gotten herself into? Think. She hurried to the bar area for a drink to steady herself and clear her head. She took a glass from the shelf and gave herself a healthy pour of Angel Envy. As she put the drink to her lips, she noticed a glass in the sink. Her hand froze. Without taking a sip, she put her bourbon down, spilling some on the bar. She was pretty damn sure she didn't leave anything there. Could it had been Jim? Someone else? In her head, her voice was yelling "get the fuck out" but her feet didn't move. She cupped her hands around her mouth and nose to slow her gasping. What should she do? Where to go? Her purse. She was still wearing it. The strap swung over her coat. Her hand shook as she reached in and grabbed her phone. Call Jim? Yes, get him back here. Hell, two people were better than one.

Her vision blurred as her thumb pressed Favorites on her cell's screen. She was tearing and it made the search for Jim's name difficult. She wiped her eyes with the sleeve of her coat and tried again. It should be easy. *Where the hell is it?* Instead of favorites she was in Contacts, then her thumb slipped to another app.

"I can't believe this is happening." She stared at her phone. "Siri call Jim."

"Tim has two numbers. Which one would you like?"

"Shit…Jim…Jim."

She was about to scream "Siri" when she heard her doorbell. It rang in rapid succession. *Oh, God.*

Chapter Thirty-One

Brandt stared at his computer screen while compiling a list of Nicole's doctors. As their phone numbers were not on the prescription bottles, he had to Google each name and hope it was the correct one, then type in their information. His back and shoulders began to ache from all the typing and research. He studied one of the last bottles searching for information. He heard footsteps and looked up. Detective Young was walking toward him. It could have been his eyes from looking at all the small print but there was something about her that he couldn't put his finger on…her hair? Her clothes?

"Looked here, you've returned. I didn't expect you back so soon."

She didn't say anything.

"I take it your hunch was wrong. Jim wasn't there or the little bitch didn't let you in."

"Don't be so smug." She dropped her purse on her desk and fell into her chair. Brandt's gaze didn't leave her. After a few seconds, she nodded. "Okay, okay, you were right. It was a waste of time. My gut was wrong." She shrugged. "How's the doc list going?"

"Slow and it's Sunday so no one is around."

Young got up and moved behind Brandt. She was near enough for him to get a whiff of her perfume…something orangey. Whoa. She never wore that before. Or did she and he didn't notice? Maybe they weren't that close. Her hand touched his shoulder. A tingle of sensations ran up his spine. Young interrupted his wanderings.

"Since I was a bad girl, let me finish the list. It's the least I can do."

"It's all right. I'm down to the last couple of bottles." He glanced at the computer screen, then back at Young. His shirt collar was already unbuttoned, and the knot of his tie pulled down. He pointed to all the medicine containers lined on his desk. "Nicole used a lot of shit. She had pills for anxiety, depression. I think this one here"—he held up the receptacle—"bipolar. Then there was birth control, blood pressure, and this one, antibiotics. A very busy and it appears, troubled young lady."

"Huh. She certainly didn't come off that way."

Brandt studied her. "What do you mean?"

"Jim, Lori, or the little bitch downstairs didn't give us that impression."

Brandt ran his hand through his hair. "Maybe they didn't know, but we didn't have this information to ask." He pointed to the medicines on his desk. "Didn't Lori work with her?"

"Ahh, yeah, I think so. We know Jim did."

Brandt smiled. "Yep, but Lori could have a different perspective. What I'm getting at is there may not have been foul play. She could have taken one too many of these."

She cocked her head. "True, but... never mind."

"What?"

"Intuition. I know, I was wrong before, but something doesn't smell right."

Brandt rubbed his chin.

"What? You're thinking of something," she asked.

"I am. We should pay Lori a visit."

"You want to go... now?"

"Just a thought. The list will be finished in a few minutes. We can try the doctors tomorrow."

Young checked her watch. "It's getting near shift change, isn't it? The captain will be pissed if we put in for overtime."

"Yeah, I guess so, but..."

She moved closer to him, her perfume almost intoxicating. "Jesus, Brandt, get a life. It's Sunday night for God's sake. Let's grab a bite. We'll get to this crap later."

Did she just make a play for me? Partners do have meals together. He was thinking too much.

He kept his eyes on her while he mulled over her offer. There definitely was a change. The way she carried herself… her…Jesus, if he'd met up with Carla last night maybe he wouldn't have noticed. The old adage "you don't eat where you crap" popped into his head.

"Tempting offer," he said.

Carla or Young. At least with Carla there were no complications. Besides, with a little luck he could have a feast of a different sort. Sunday was usually slow for her.

"Nah, thanks, you go ahead. I'll finish up. See you tomorrow."

* * *

Young grabbed her purse from her desk. Another five minutes of playing policewoman. "All right, Brandt, don't burn the midnight oil. Get the hell out of here, sooner than later. See you tomorrow."

He gave her a half-hearted wave and turned back to his computer. She walked down the stairs to the first floor, exchanged greetings with another officer, and returned to her car in the parking lot. She sat back in her seat, relieved on the one hand and keyed up on the other. How long can she keep the pretense from Brandt? Jesus, it was a stupid idea to ask him to have dinner. She was sure he saw the invitation as something else. He was right. Dumb, dumb, dumb. What a hell of a day. Going through Nicole's apartment as if she'd never been there, then acting the tough dick to Neve while visualizing her naked body left her with much unfinished business.

Charlie started her car and drove out of the parking lot. She didn't feel like going home. Nothing much happening there. Try Neve again? She toyed with that idea. Neve was probably as rattled as she. Neve's "change of plans" text could have meant—in that moment. Nicole often said, "Neve is flighty but has a lot of energy when directed." Charlie knew of the energy and that thought sealed the deal.

Traffic was light as usual on a Sunday evening. Her musings went between what may be awaiting at Neve's place and Brandt's description of Nicole. Charlie knew Nicole took medication. After all, she was a detective and did a little snooping after one of those exquisite nights that started with Nicole and later included Neve. Charlie had gotten up from Nicole's bed and headed to the bathroom. She used the time to check it out. Discreetly hidden behind bottles of perfumes in a cabinet were two containers of pills whose labels Charlie recognized. One was for anxiety and the other was a muscle relaxant. There wasn't time to scope out the other bottles now arrayed on Brandt's desk.

Nicole, though, hid whatever deficiencies she had. She was always in control. She knew what she wanted and was smooth at persuasion. She was one focused woman. Charlie considered herself no pushover, but...here she was on the prowl for Neve. The bargain between the three of them was a drug she couldn't get enough of. Nicole used Charlie's insatiable drive as she used Neve's growing dependence and longing. That must have been the same way for Jim and anyone else who had contact with Nicole. She was a quick study of someone's weakness and mined it for her use. Charlie hesitated as to where her logic was leading. It wasn't Nicole who was fucked up, but her, Neve, and the others who were sucked into Nicole's web.

Shit. She reached for her purse and grabbed her emergency pack of Marlboros. Her car was one of the few that still had a lighter, but no ashtray. She lit up and took a deep drag. Damn, she'd never wanted to give up smoking in the first place. She cracked the window to let the smoke out as she drove.

What did Nicole get out of it? Charlie smiled in the darkened car and tapped her free hand on the steering wheel...certainly satisfaction. That girl put out and enjoyed it. Christ, she was so, so, good. Then why have Neve there? Of course, she added more spice, but the pleasure would have been the same. Nicole, though…damn…She closed her eyes for a split-second, forming a recurrent thought. She took another puff. Her hand grew clammy clutching the wheel. Was all that oohing and aahing a series of great performances? A picture of her, Neve, Jim, and the others formed, hanging on separate strings, vying to be Nicole's one and only. She hated that conclusion. She fought it. She fought it for some time. She had told herself it was impossible for Nicole to be that good an actress. Nicole gave not only physically but spiritually so much of herself. How could it be only an act?

Charlie felt her eyes tearing. *Grow up*, she told herself. She dealt with liars and worse as a cop. What was the truth? The sound of her tires seemed to affirm what she damn well knew.

She neared the Gold Coast neighborhood at about 6:45 p.m. It was never too early to begin the hunt for a parking space. It was the one big drawback to living there, besides the expense. Then again, everything had a cost.

Chapter Thirty-Two

Skinny went through the alley after leaving the broad's house. He reached his car and got in, then called his boss. "Mr. Hill, I did what you asked."

"And...?"

"Didn't find anything, but I did scare the shit out of her. She knew someone had been in the house."

"Spare me the details."

"No problem. Anything else?"

"Let me think. Yes, go back but this time ring the bell. Introduce yourself that you're from Human Resources and collect her ID and shit. Her name is Lori...not sure of her last. Tell her to be at HR no later than ten o'clock a.m. tomorrow morning."

"Got it."

"Wait, Skinny, you there?"

"Uh-huh."

"Get her to talk as to where she was today as well as any dirt on her good-for-nothing boyfriend, Jim."

"Ah...by any..."

"Skinny, no details, remember."

"Yes sir, Mr. Hill. I'll contact you after."

"Good."

* * *

Hill stuck his phone back in his pocket. He was parked on Seminary and Lincoln Ave. His instructions from JK's text was to wait until a black Lincoln limo with license plate ZZZ arrived. He then was to hand the photos of Jim and Nicole's tell-all book to the driver. Every now and then he'd check the rear and side view mirror for any sign of the car. His eyes wandered from there to the clock on the dash as well as the watch on his arm. Waiting was such a pain in the ass. The limo should have been here. He turned on the radio and looked at his watch again. Besides the hand-off, he figured an hour and change had passed since he left Herman and the building. Most likely, Herman would have nothing more to report. The trespasser, he was sure, had left and his suspicion that it was Lori…something or other, made sense. Other than Jim, who else would be nosing around Nicole's office? Hill knew Lori was questioned by the police and as long as the heat was also on Jim, they continued to be the prime suspects. Nicole's tell-all had the answers Lori wanted. Too bad, he got there first.

Was Nicole murdered? He laughed; for the moment, the important thing was she was dead, end of story. The bitch was too ambitious and clever. She reached too high too fast. Nicole went through several higher-ranking people, including Jim, and had her sights on a vice-presidency if not more. That meant some top-ranking person or persons in the hierarchy of the company were compromised and that would be bad for the firm. He gazed out his driver's side window as the thought rattled around his brain. JK? The Chairman of the Board and CEO? He shook his head. Too much risk for him. Hill leaned back and pressed a button for more heat.

Hell, he had cleaned up enough shit for JK involving women. JK wasn't very discreet when it came to that. Money, a whisper in the right ear of scandal and if necessary, a little

physical intimidation were Hill's time-honored ingredients. It worked. JK's sterling reputation was never tainted.

Hill glanced at his outside mirror for the limo. Still nothing. He rubbed his face and sighed. He turned the radio down as it blared some stupid ass ad for female leakage. Huh, did JK ever refer to Nicole in that way? Jesus, JK was aware that she was banging people. He told Hill to watch the situation and make sure it didn't get out of hand.

That's what he did all right. He had Skinny do a dive into her apartment. Hill found, through Skinny's good work, that Nicole was a walking pharmaceutical. He read up on some of the anti-depressives, then approached Nicole in her office.

Hill scanned the outside street—more wait.

He remembered it was early evening and most of the staff had left for the day. Nicole was in the bathroom. The door open. He watched as she brushed her hair, then applied lipstick.

"You like the show?" she asked.

Hill had his hands in his pants pockets, cleared his throat. "Yeah, very nice. Looks like you're going somewhere."

"Dinner." She looked at her Cartier watch. "I'm running a little late. What can I do for you?"

"Do you know who I am?"

She stopped and glanced in his direction. "A man who thinks he's important."

"That's right. I'm JK's assistant."

"You are?" She smiled. Her white teeth gleamed.

"We or I should say, he, knows what you are doing, and you need to stop."

"Oh really." She stepped closer to him. He could smell her perfume. She whispered, "What am I doing.... Mr. Hill?"

"How did you..."

She put a finger to her lips.

Her blouse left little to the imagination as she stepped even closer.

"I believe in this company, Mr. Hill, and I want to make it the best there is. I am very capable and given the opportunity I can..."

Hill felt she cast a spell. He was about to violate his own rules.

"Rewards, Mr. Hill. Work well done should always be rewarded."

A car horn blared. Hill flinched. The damn Lincoln pulled up to his driver's side. Hill lowered his window and gave the photos and Nicole's tell-all to an outstretched hand. The limo's tinted window made it impossible to see who it was. Seconds later it drove off. Hill remained in his seat and watched the limo's taillights disappear. He stared out the front window and his thoughts shot back to *that* day.

He would have made a move, but she laughed. The spell, broken.

"I have to go now. I'll try to behave." She winked.

She left him standing in her office.

It was sometime later, a week, two, JK called and asked for a report on Nicole. Hill told him about the drugs and about confronting her but left a few details out. He also informed JK how taking one of her medications, Nardil, along with wine could be fatal but would leave no trace. JK asked why was that something he should know. Hill explained in case of legal repercussions. The way Nicole carried on, the company could face liability. JK didn't respond.

Hill glanced at the clock on the dash. It was night and besides being tired, the memory of that meeting with Nicole awoke what he had denied himself for too long. "Work well done should be rewarded." A fine quote and there was no question he'd done everything JK ever asked. It was time to cash in, and he knew just where.

Chapter Thirty-Three

The name *Siri* stuck in Lori's throat. She couldn't get the word out much less a command. The doorbell went off again. The sound no longer a bell tone to her, but a siren. The shrillness of it drilled her ears and made her step toward the door. She prayed the noise to stop, but every few seconds the bastard continued the assault. She kept silent and placed her hand on the doorknob. She could hear her heart pound as she stood on her toes and looked through the peephole. A man stood outside. She didn't recognize him. She pressed against the door, with the absurd idea if she didn't answer he'd go away. It didn't happen. This man, tired of the bell, began to knock. It was as if he knew she was home. Drops of sweat streaked down her face. *What to do?* Her knees buckled. She stopped herself from falling. *Enough.*

"Who the fuck is there?" she yelled.

The knocking stopped...the cannons ceased firing. Time stood still until he responded.

"I'm from Human Resources. We need to speak."

HR? On a Sunday? Jesus, the word gets out fast. "Jim isn't home."

"Are you Lori?"

She wiped her face with her sleeve. *He wants to speak to me? Why?* She cleared her throat. "What do you want?"

"Sorry for all the racket I caused. It's been a long day. Listen, Lori, we can't do this through the door. It's routine. A coworker of yours has died, and the company has been informed that the police questioned you. We need to talk. Nothing to worry about."

His tone was calm, non-threatening, like asking if you'd want cream in your coffee. *Maybe I've blown this all out of proportion. After all, I did work with Nicole and the police did question me. Any company would be curious as to my role, especially since Jim had an affair with her.*

She heard herself say, "Okay" and unlocked the door. The peephole view didn't do the man justice. He was large, not fat, but big. "Do you have ID?"

"Sure," he said. There was no chance of pushing him out if things went south.

He smiled and reached into his jean jacket. He opened a leather case and flashed a card. She saw a glimpse of the company emblem but didn't catch a name. "You did that too fast. I couldn't read it."

He stuffed the case in his shirt pocket, nodded, and proceeded to enter. "Let's sit." He pointed to the couch in the sunken living room.

She had no choice but to follow. She took a seat near the edge, he in a chair across from her.

"Alex," Skinny said by way of introduction. "How long have you been with the company?"

"About five years."

"What division?"

She was about to answer then stopped. "You mean Jim?"

"No, not him. You."

"Don't you already have this information?"

She saw his eyes flutter. It happened almost imperceptibly, despite his voice staying calm and almost melodious. "Just routine. Stupid, but it's what the company wants."

"Uh-huh."

"How long have you and Jim been together?" He turned his head, glancing at the first-floor layout.

"Something like five years."

"Did you know Jim and your supervisor, Nicole, were having an affair?"

"Not at the time. No… not until the other day when the cops came. I—I…" She looked away, her hand gripping her phone.

"Really? You had no idea?"

She shook her head. "Dumb, I guess. I didn't see it coming."

Alex leaned forward. "Yeah?" His response was sharp and disbelieving.

"I'm not lying. It came as a shock. I found out after I learned she died."

He paused, then looked away from her. "Is that what you told the police? It's important for the company to know. Liability and all that."

"Lia—" She moved her shoulder. "Yeah, more or less. I don't remember exactly. The last few days have been a fog."

Alex shifted his weight. "Where's Jim?"

"I threw him out this morning."

"You have no idea where he went?"

The man made a home out of the chair. One question after another like a machine gun, but he wrote nothing down. It dawned on her that was strange. Maybe he was secretly recording her? Wasn't that illegal? She began to limit her answers to "yes" and "no." Her mouth felt as dry as sand in the desert. She needed a drink…water, booze, anything for a breather.

She held up the palm of her hand. "Stop. I need something to drink." She rose from her seat, the phone still clutched in her hand.

"I'll take that."

"What? What will you take?"

"Your phone."

She slunk back. "My phone? Why?"

A broad smile crossed his face. "Why do you think?"

She shook her head. "I—I don't know. It's my phone."

"You're not understanding. I'm not asking. I'm telling you."

She didn't need to be a detective. Her phone not only contained who she'd called but where she'd been. She glanced from the monster of a man to her phone. "I'm calling the police. Get out."

He bounded out of his chair. He moved quickly for a big man. His meaty large paws gripped her hand.

"You're hurting… stop…"

He slapped her hard across her face. The phone dropped out of her grasp. He quickly picked it off the couch cushion, then stood over her. "You're trouble and a liar. The company doesn't want people like you. Not good for the brand." He paused. "You went to the office today…didn't you? You went into places you had no right to be?"

She rubbed her face where she had been slapped. "Get out, get out." She was screaming.

Skinny reacted. He dropped the phone, then covered her mouth with one hand and grabbed her throat with the other. She squirmed, kicked, her eyes wide. She tried to bite his fingers but failed. The pressure on her throat grew. It became hard to breathe. "Please don't please do…" she begged with her eyes. She pictured a fish hooked from the sea as it fought for air that was rightfully hers. She flopped on the dock. There was no more air. Her struggle ceased.

* * *

The moment Lori screamed a switch turned on and Skinny went on the attack. This wasn't what he or Mr. Hill wanted, but the bitch crossed the line. She almost bit him. Damn her. She was stronger than he thought. The pressure on her throat should have killed her minutes ago. Damn, the hellcat wouldn't go down. "Die already," he muttered. As Lori's movement slowed, he heard what he thought was the doorbell. He eased the pressure and listened. Holy Jesus, someone was at the door. He looked at Lori who'd stopped moving, but he wasn't sure if she was dead. No time to waste. He recovered Lori's phone and as quietly as he could headed out the back door. Once in the alley, he forced himself to walk and not run. He figured people in this neighborhood wouldn't take notice. He eased out of his jean jacket and at the corner dropped it in a dumpster. His pace quickened reaching the street. His car was in sight, another forty feet or so. After opening his vehicle's door, he glanced over to Lori's home, five houses down from him. He could see there was a person at her door. He dipped his body into the driver's seat, grabbed his locksmith jacket, then took several large breaths. Should he leave or wait? His eyes focused on his rear-view mirror. Where the fuck did he go?

Chapter Thirty-Four

Hill left the parking space on Seminary and Lincoln. He checked his phone while driving for any updates from Skinny and Herman. Not likely that Herman would come through and find something on the videos. But Skinny…he was damn sure Skinny would confirm his hunch about Lori. He furled his brow. Skinny was very persuasive. As for the little bitch, Neve, well, once daddy read Nicole's book, Neve's days living her care-free life were numbered. The boss will cut her off… Such a shame. He made a *tsk tsk* sound and stepped on the gas. His self-appointed reward would soon be in his grasp. As Nicole so aptly advised…good work should always be recognized. Indeed.

It didn't take long to reach the Gold Coast. Parking was always a bitch, but luck was with him. He found a space on Dearborn and Burton—three to four blocks from Neve's. Once parked, he turned his phone off. He should have done it before but no need to compound the mistake. Skinny or Herman can wait an hour or two…better to be cautious than reckless.

He turned his attention to his prey and wondered if the spoiled brat was waiting for him. He left little doubt he'd be coming back. Did she change clothes or keep the outfit that had barely covered her. He couldn't decide which he preferred. But then it didn't matter, because he could order her to do whatever he wanted.

He liked that thought. He reveled in control, of other people's lives in his hands. He was God with a small "g."

His walk was brisk in the early evening, purposeful but not brazen. As far as any fallout from Neve's old man, he doubted Neve had cards left to play. JK hated being ignored. It was visceral with him. He had warned his daughter to buckle down and behave. Nicole's tell-all sealed Neve's fate. It was like having a royal flush in his hand. Neve knew he thad Nicole's book. His threat was the hammer over her head. What Neve didn't know was he'd already given it to JK. He looked forward to disclosing that little tidbit when he finished with her—a coup de grâce after his happy ending. A warm feeling of giddiness swept through him. He flung open Neve's building's front door and walked into the small foyer. He didn't bother to ring her apartment—he had copied Nicole's keys months ago. He had a young man's surge of energy as the elevator clanged its way to the second floor. An hour or two of rewards—paid in full.

* * *

Neve readied herself for Hill. She changed back into her thong and a cream-colored blouse that tied in the front. She caught a glimpse of herself in her bedroom mirror. *This should get his dick's attention.*

Neve was much aware of Hill's reputation. She'd overheard many of her daddy's conversations. Hill was one mean sonofabitch. Well, he was in for a big surprise. She didn't doubt that Nikki kept a tell-all. Although Nikki gave the appearance of being free and easy, Neve came slowly to realize that that was not the case. Most things Nikki did were calculated—who she saw and slept with had a purpose. Neve grasped that Nikki had reasons for having sex with at least three of the people. Jim was Nikki's bitch. He'd do whatever she wanted when she wanted. Nothing was out of bounds. Charlie's position as a cop would be used when it was needed. It was money in the bank. As for herself, hmm, she was the boss's daughter. Holy shit, she didn't see it before. What if the unknown man in Nikki's life was… She buried her head in her hands. Impossible, too horrible to think. She fanned herself with her hand. *No way. He wouldn't…no.* She brushed away that thought. She had to get ready for Hill. She went into the dining room and opened her china cabinet. In one of the drawers tucked away in the back was a stash of pills in an envelope stolen from Nikki. She wasn't precise as to the particular names but was aware they were anti-depressives. She had Googled what the interaction was with the medicine and alcohol. She would take the chance.

It was past six in the evening. She felt her adrenalin pumping. The sonofabitch was near. She knew it…felt it. She went to her wine rack and opened a bottle, then poured herself a glass, then another, and another. She left one for him. She was feeling mellow as the wine began its work. With her glass in hand, she went to the door and opened it a crack. She heard the elevator's whine. He was coming. She went back to the living room and grabbed the two pills taken from the envelope. *Here goes.* They went down easy as she finished her third, or maybe it was the fourth. She didn't give a fuck. She hoped she'd pass out before Hill did anything. In her mind it would be druggus interruptus with a call from a hospital to Daddy.

Chapter Thirty-Five

Charlie had found parking on Clark two blocks south of North Avenue. It was a bit of a distance, but what the hell. The hike would clear her head. People were all around waiting for Ubers or cabs, about to go to dinner…the air cold and crisp. This Gold Coast area was certainly the place to be. It was a little upper West Side New York, fused with the Champs-Élysées. So different from where she grew up or now lived. *Damn, to have money.*

The walk chased thoughts of Nicole aside. All that dribble in the car went poof. Charlie knew what she wanted and if Brandt didn't want to, despite it being a stupid idea, Neve was the answer. What if she wasn't there?

Charlie stopped for a moment, then it came to her. She misunderstood Neve's "change of plans" text. She thought back to earlier in the day when she and Brandt were in the apartment. She had a strong hunch some man was there, probably Jim. She was blessed or cursed with a keen sense of smell, and she smelled a "him." She smiled at the thought. Brandt would think her crazy if she told him but she was right. Her gut told her it was Jim, and Neve wanted him for herself. What better way of not being disturbed than to text Charlie to get lost. Neve had learned from her mistress, Nicole.

Tonight will make up for Nicole and all the shit she'd had Charlie go through. She almost laughed at how much she'd wanted to be Nicole's one and only.

Charlie was now a block from Neve's apartment. Her heartbeat grew faster and there was energy in her step. The picture of Neve and her in bed flashed through her mind. *How fuck'n exciting.* She stopped at the corner for the light. What if Jim was still there? What if Neve was too tired? *What if…give it a rest.* The light was about to turn green. Should she send Neve a text or just show up? She went for surprise, crossing the street.

She saw Neve's building. Her second-floor apartment was ablaze with light. *So much for change of plans. Neve had indeed learned from Nicole.* A pleasurable surge filled Charlie with anticipation. She started up the walkway, her head contemplating unimaginable delights. She paid no attention to a man who walked out the front door of the building until he brushed by her without an apology. "Hey, watch it, bud," she said. She glanced back as the older-looking man disappeared. No matter, most likely someone who knew the first-floor tenants. He certainly wasn't Neve's type. Then scolded herself for being so self-absorbed. She was, after all, a cop and should pay more attention to her surroundings. She looked down the street but whoever that was, was gone. She sighed. *Let's not spoil the evening.* She entered the building, then rang Neve's apartment, but there was no response. Maybe Neve had her ten-thousand-dollar stereo system on and couldn't hear. She'd done that before. Charlie waited, rang again. *Ach, that pleasure-seeking bitch.* She dipped into her purse and took out a set of keys. Seconds later, she was in the elevator clanging her way to Neve's floor.

"Neve? You slut." Charlie called out, standing in front of Neve's apartment door. "Open up." She giggled at her own humor. "Neve?" *Jesus.* She put her ear to the door and listened. Music, although she couldn't tell what kind. *Neve must be having fun.* She tried the door. She had warned Neve on several occasions to make sure to use the lock, but…the carefreeness of youth.

Charlie stood in Neve's entryway. Hard rock blaring. The electric guitars' sound bouncing off the floorboards. "Neve?" It seemed every light was on. Charlie went to the console in the living room and pushed the power button to Off. The apartment…silent. "Neve, it's me, Charlie."

The bedroom door was half-closed. Charlie pushed it open. Neve laid on the bedcover. Charlie took in Neve's pose. The shapely bare legs leading to her gorgeous, perfectly formed uncovered ass waiting for Charlie's hands and lips. "Oh, you beautiful girl." She unbuttoned her coat and stepped toward the bed. Neve didn't move. "Neve? Oh, we're playing games again."

Charlie heard the faint click of a door somewhere in the apartment. She drew her gun holstered at her side. Stealthily, she went from the bedroom to the front hallway and pulled the door open. The elevator cage hadn't moved. She edged towards the stairwell but saw no one. Her hands were cold gripping her weapon. Maybe she hadn't heard anything.

She returned to Neve's apartment and locked the front door. No, she'd definitely caught something. The apartment was still. With her gun at her side, she searched the other rooms, then went into the kitchen. *The fuck'n backdoor, of course. As* quietly as possible, she took a position behind the door. It was easy to see the lock was not engaged. *Shit.* She took a deep breath grabbed the handle, and swung the door open. She edged out to the landing and in a crouch walked down several stairs listening for any sound. Nothing. She followed the dimly lit staircase to ground level. A steel door led to the outside. She turned the handle and pushed the door a crack. The cool night air hit her as she enlarged her opening until she had the view of the alley. Nothing to see except trash cans—no persons or vehicles—only night.

* * *

Jim hurried down the alley. *Oh, my God, oh God,* he kept saying. *I can't believe…Neve. Shit.* Several more obscenities came rolling out of his mouth. He was hot and sweaty, then cold. The wind knifed through him. What to do? Who to call? Lori? Would she believe him? He patted his pocket. Thank God he still had his phone. He had to find a place. Somewhere to sit and think this through, but his concentration was interrupted by the dog crap and strewn garbage he needed to avoid. At the alley's mouth, he turned right toward State and Division Streets. He breathed a little easier as he blended in with the hustle and bustle of people on their way to their evening's affairs. On the corner he spotted what in his neighborhood would be considered a greasy spoon but in the Gold Coast, a bistro, with commensurate prices. He ducked in and was immediately seated with a view of the street and front door. A busboy filled a glass of water and set it on his table. Before he could reach for the glass a waitress appeared.

"What can I get you?" a girl wearing a ponytail asked. She seemed no older than a high school kid.

His eyes danced from the chalk board for specials hanging on the wall to the door and then the window. "Could you give me a minute or so?"

"Sure, absolutely. I'll be back."

As soon as she left, he grabbed his phone from his pocket. He used both hands to type in Lori's number. It appeared on the screen in seconds. "Lori, Lori it's me…" There was no sound. Was his cell working? Damn, he didn't press the round phone icon. The full consequence of what the call may do hit him. Should he? Who else was there? His thumb pressed the button. He heard the clicks, then the buzz. After several rings, a connection was made.

"Lori? You there? Lori?" Silence. He checked the screen and saw seconds tick by. "Lori? Come on, answer, for God's sake."

"This ain't Lori, bub. You got the wrong number." The voice was deep and male. The line went dead.

Chapter Thirty-Six

Whirley got up to look at the clock near her bed. It was past five in the afternoon. Damn, most of Sunday was gone. She balanced herself on her arm and gazed around the room. She spotted her last night's jeans on the floor along with her cute little jacket. *Must have been a hell of an evening. She pulled herself into a sitting position and remembered. Oh yeah, Jimbo. Surprise. The chump was so disappointed. The look on his face. It was the perfect screw.*

She swung her legs from the bed to the floor and went to find and count her money. She eyed the two items of clothing and tried to recall which one was stuffed with cash. She picked up her coat first and was rewarded—ten folded Franklins. She got paid well for a night's work, and she didn't even put out. It was a crazy world. She dropped the bills on her bedside table and checked her phone. A missed call from Brandt early in the day. Oh well, better she slept through it. She would have been too tired to give him what he wanted.

She stretched her arms over her head and decided it was as good a time as any to take her shower. The steam and hot water would be just the thing.

She usually sang while showering but the melodies wandered off to last night. Jimbo intruded. *No happy ending for him.* She got a laugh out of it. There rarely were second thoughts about her jobs. She provided a service and wasn't responsible for ramifications. Sex, as she saw it, was like religion. It could provide solace, contentment, and love, or be misused and lead to all sorts of bad things. It all depended on who and the why.

She turned the shower off. *Where the hell is my towel? Damn it, I'm freezing.* The cold ruined the mellowness. Her teeth chattered and, hugging her body, she found the towel hanging behind the door several feet away. She grabbed it and wrapped herself in its warmth. Once settled, her thoughts meandered to Jimbo again. He was like a ripe apple ready to be plucked from the tree. She didn't twist his arm or any other part of him. He'd taken a look at her and began to sing her hymns. He wanted rapture and thought she'd provide it. The belief was all in his head. She dug into her makeup bag and carefully applied eye shadow. Why was she hired as a lure and why the pictures? She held her eyeliner pencil in the air, then brought it down to rest on the counter. She bent closer to the mirror, then straightened. Why should she care? Questions were inappropriate and darn right dangerous in her line of work. No questions, no emotional involvement—hurray for more business.

She finished her eyes, then blow-dried her hair. The last touch was applying lipstick. She chose a darker shade of red. That done, she walked to her closet and picked a black cashmere sweater to complement the jeans on the floor. In the full-length mirror hanging on her bedroom door, she checked herself out from all angles. Satisfied with the look, she was ready to step out and grab what the evening brought.

* * *

Brandt rang Lori's door. He glanced to his left and then his right. Nothing out of the ordinary to see. No one was walking or driving down the street. He pressed the bell again. "Hello? Anyone there?" He leaned against the door and identified what he thought were footsteps. He strained to listen, but the sound disappeared. He straightened. Seconds later there was the *thunk* of a door opening or closing. He tried the door handle. It was locked. *Must be in the rear.* He hurried around the garage through the side yard, hugging the outline of the home. "Police," he yelled and drew his weapon. When he reached the back, nothing was disturbed, and no one was outside. He stood and listened, stepping toward the alley. It was quiet. He holstered his gun and after looking around again, he tried the rear door. Jesus, with a twist of the knob it opened. He walked into the kitchen. "Ms. Knight, Jim, this is Detective Brandt, put your hands above your head." He grabbed his automatic and made his way toward the front. The sunken living room came into view. A woman sprawled on the couch with her head drooped to the side.

"Lori? Ms. Knight?" He quickened his step and reholstered his gun. Her eyes were open. Her mouth gaped. He checked her neck for a pulse but knew there wouldn't be one. "Holy shit." He raced up the stairs to the second floor and searched the rooms. Nobody was there and the area appeared undisturbed. He returned to the main floor and reached for his phone to call his district. He identified himself, then gave the information to the desk sergeant. "Put out an APB for a Jim 'James' O'Dell. There's a picture of him in my file on my desk. I'll wait for the cavalry to arrive."

He didn't want to touch or disturb anything. He kept his phone in his hand and stared at the body, then snapped several pictures.

Brandt had done many death investigations. The process was, in a way, simple. If the who, when, where, why, and how were answered the case was solved. The *how, when,* and *where* did not appear to be a problem here. The *why* was also not difficult to glean. Jimbo. He was the prime suspect. Hell, the *fucker* had an affair. Lori caught him. They argued about that. There were lesser reasons why people killed others. Or while that scenario brewed, Jim confessed to Lori he murdered Nicole. Lori then threatened to go to the cops. Brandt glanced at the front door and several of the windows...no forced entry. It was, Brandt believed, a good start as to "why." Brandt rubbed his chin, then took more pictures of the living room. As he snapped the frames, he remembered Detective Young hadn't found Jim when she returned to Neve's place later in the afternoon. Jim may have never left this house.

Brandt moved towards the bar, picturing Jim. As he recalled, Jim wasn't that big of a guy. Nor did he appear to have the kind of strength needed to strangle someone. A point for the suspect. Brandt slowly nodded, though that didn't rule it out either.

At the bar, Brandt saw an open bottle of bourbon, then a glass in the sink. He refrained from touching the tumbler, although that was his first instinct. *That sucker better be bagged and not lost like the brandy glass in Nicole's apartment.* Instead, he took more photos. When he finished, he checked his watch. *The sirens should be coming in the next few minutes. H*e should call Detective Young and have her meet him here. *Shit, it's her case too.* He rubbed his neck after punching in her number. Should he hit Call? They both were off the clock. He'd come here to ask Lori about Nicole's drugs…on his own time. Young, he believed, had other things cooking. He glanced at the digits on his screen. *What the hell? If I don't call there'll be too much explaining.* He punched the icon.

She didn't answer.

Chapter Thirty-Seven

Charlie returned to Neve's bedroom. Neve hadn't moved. She laid there as she had done numerous times before. "Come on, Neve, stop fucking around. Too much has happened."Charlie stared at the bed, hoping, praying for some, any, sign of life. "Okay, Neve, you've scared the shit out of me. You win. You got me." Charlie looked away for a second or two. "Did that guy I chased tire you out? Come on, move. Do something." Tears formed as reality of the situation hit Charlie. She swayed. "You're not… dead. Oh God please…"Nausea bubbled from her stomach to her throat. "This can't be happening. Just can't," she repeated. She fought her emotions and took several deep breaths. "Neve?" Charlie's hand trembled as she touched Neve's leg. Christ. The skin was cool but not cold. Was Neve, alive? Charlie drew a sharp breath at the shock of the discovery. Call an ambulance. Neve had to get help. Charlie whipped out her phone. "Hang in there…9-1-1."

She stopped the transmission before it went through. There would be questions and more questions. Her phone would be traced. Her location revealed. What was she doing in Neve's apartment? What was she thinking? She had to find another way.

"Where's your phone? Neve, your phone." Charlie rummaged the table by the bed, then kneeled and searched the floor. "Goddamn it. Neve, your phone."

She stood, breathing hard. She had to decide—risk losing her plaything, or her job. Who did she envision herself to be—a cop, a detective with a hell of a future. She erased the 911 from her screen and ran out of the apartment, down the stairs to the first floor. She rang the bell, then pounded on the door. "Call an ambulance, hurry, call 911." Charlie didn't wait for someone to answer. She rushed out the building and slowed her jog to a walk. Once on the street, she wrestled with hoping the neighbor heard and the fear she'd get caught. Her ticker was thumping hard. Drops of sweat drooped from her hairline despite shivering.

She was a block from Neve's when her cell, still in her hand, went off. "Holy shit." She stopped and attempted to focus on the number, wiping away tears from the cold and wind. *That number, I know it.* It took a second or two—Brandt.

* * *

Jim sat at the table in the restaurant fidgeting with his cell. About an hour ago, maybe it was more or less, he had returned to Neve's apartment by the alley stairs. She hadn't relocked her back door. That was Neve. One minute, security conscious; the next, something else caught her mind. Thank God he didn't say anything when he came in, although with her stereo blasting, she most likely wouldn't have heard. He got close to her bedroom but stopped when he heard a *thwack* like someone smacking bare skin. A second or two later that sound was followed by, "You bitch!" in an angry male voice. It had to be Hill. His voice carried above the music, calling Neve every name in the book and then some. Jim crept back to the kitchen area. He didn't know how long he hid until he caught a glimpse of Hill stalking out the bedroom toward the front door. Jim waited several seconds, then raced to Neve. She lay on her stomach, her top rolled to her neck, leaving the rest of her body naked on the bed. "Neve, are you all right?"

She didn't answer.

He touched her leg. Her skin felt cool. "Jesus, Neve, don't play. What did Hill do to you?" He stood over her and was about to dial 911, when the air or something changed and almost simultaneously the music shut off. Jim heard a woman's voice calling, "Neve." That's when he got the hell out of there. He had to call Lori. He had to tell her; warn her. Instead, a man answered her number. His hands shook as he concentrated on his phone in front of him. He had to calm down.

150

"I'm Annie. I'll be your server tonight. What can I get you?"

It took a moment for Jim to recognize someone was speaking. He glanced at his phone, then looked away. "What was that?"

The waitress in her chirpy voice repeated her lines.

Jim held up his hand and gestured *just a minute*, then quickly examined the menu. "I... eh... Jesus, I...don't..." He looked up. "Get me a scotch. Make it a double."

"What kind?"

"Christ, whatever." He thought for a moment. "Johnny Walker."

"Black or red?"

"Ah...black."

"Rocks or neat?"

"Another question?"

"I want you to be satisfied."

"Are you old enough to serve this stuff?"

She blushed. "I'm twenty-seven. Rocks or neat?"

"Twenty-seven? Wow. You sure?" He took a long look at her. She was beginning to have his full attention.

"Yep. Graduated Columbia College two years ago. People think I'm in my teens but I'm not. I work at Steppenwolf when I'm not doing this."

"Impressive...an actress." He looked at her nametag. "Well, Annie, let me know the show you're in. I'd love to see it." His immediate crisis being edged aside.

"I do the lighting."

"Oh... must be interesting."

"A lot of technical stuff." She looked over at the other tables. "I'll get your drink. Rocks?"

"Sure." He watched her yell his order to the bartender. *Twenty-seven? She's older than Neve. Hmmm.* He slapped himself for having wandering thoughts. This was no time to get into another woman's pants. Although, her place could be somewhere to stay tonight. He shook his head. He must be nuts. He picked up his phone and stared at the number he called. It had been Lori's. How could a man answer? Could she have changed it that quickly? Jesus, life was moving way too fast.

Annie set the drink on the table. "Will there be anything else?"

Jim's eyes were watery. She must have sensed something was wrong. She lingered, then broke Jim's silence. "We have great burgers. It'd go super with the scotch."

Jim glanced back at her. "Yeah?"

"Get it with cheddar on our toasted pretzel bun. You can't go wrong."

He sighed and lifted his drink. "If you say so."

"Medium?"

"Huh?"

"The burger?"

"Oh, okay." He swallowed, then coughed as the booze hit his throat. After several seconds of hacking, he signaled he was all right and put his glass down.

"Drink some water." She waited until he did so.

"Thanks," he was finally able to say. He picked his scotch up again. "Scotch and water, you know they go together." This time it went down smooth. He felt the warmth. His nerves calming.

She waited until he put his drink down, then glanced around and said in one breath, "You'll want it with lettuce, tomato, and onion. You're cute. I get off at twelve."

Jim took the invitation nonchalantly as if it happened all the time. He looked at his watch, then slushed the ice in his drink. *Holy shit.* "That's a few hours from now. I'll eat and drink slow."

She smiled and turned toward the kitchen.

* * *

Whirley stopped at a bistro off State and Division. She thought it would be wise to get a bite before hitting the bars along the same drag. Even though it was Sunday, that didn't stop the action on Division Street. She stopped short when she looked through the window and saw Jimbo. "What the fuck." Would he recognize her?

She didn't have her long blonde wig. Her natural dark hair was short and cropped closely to her scalp. The look was sort of butch but not quite. Should she chance it? It could be fun to watch what he did. If he'd put two and two together. She studied him for another few seconds. Damn, he seemed to be alone. He probably wouldn't. His eyes when they looked up were focused on her tits and ass.

The other question that popped into her head was, why he was in this part of town. She knew he lived somewhere far north and had a long-time girlfriend. "Had" could explain the why he was on Division and State. His now maybe ex may not have been too open-minded.

Decision time. She shrugged; this could be intriguing. Besides, she was hungry.

Chapter Thirty-Eight

Charlie got into her vehicle. What the hell did Brandt want? Did he reconsider and want a booty call? That couldn't be right. That wasn't Brandt's manner, though she really didn't know what his style was. Everyone had secrets. Nicole, Neve, herself. Neve. Jesus, was she alive? Crap, why worry about Brandt when Neve may be dead. No, Neve can't be. She took some shit, that's all. Neve's a kid and knows nothing about drugs. At that age, Neve believed she was invincible and none of that bad stuff would happen.

Charlie grabbed her Marlboros from her purse. She hit the pack on the steering wheel and plucked a cigarette. Her hand shook as she lit it and inhaled deeply. She followed her exhaled smoke curling to the ceiling of her car and stared at the extinguished dome light. She squeezed her eyes shut for a moment. The neighbor…the neighbor called. They phoned for an ambulance. That's the way it went down. Neve was rushed to a hospital, and she'll be all right. The neighbor…please God. She wiped a tear from her face. *Look at me.* A fuck'n cop crying. If Brandt saw her now.

She started her car and drove toward the Kennedy Expressway. After about fifteen minutes, she worked up enough nerve. "Call Brandt," she ordered her vehicle's technology. Seconds later, Brandt answered.

"Hello, Young?"

"What's up?" Her voice restrained.

"Lori Knight's been murdered."

"Oh, my God. How? When?"

"I found her about forty-five minutes ago. She was strangled. The ET techs are here. There doesn't seem to be any signs of break-in. It doesn't take rocket science to figure out who probably did it. How soon can you get here?"

Young rested her hand with the cigarette on the steering wheel. Jim killed Lori? If he did, who ran out Neve's back door? Not that she was sure it was Jim, but it was as good a guess as any. She checked for expressway road signs. "ETA about twenty minutes, maybe ten, traffic is light."

"I'll be waiting."

* * *

Hill slammed the door of his car. Rushing from Neve's apartment had left him out of breath. The bitch! How could she? Dare she? Make it seem he tried to murder her. Rape her. He slapped his forehead. The list of crimes could go on. But if she didn't wake? He caught his breath. If she died, then no one would know he was there. Most likely it would be what's-his-name… Jim as the prime suspect. *Yeah, that's it. Jim.* It made sense. Neve and Nicole had similar deaths. Should he go back and make sure? No, no, what was he thinking. Why chance someone seeing? Luck only held for so long. He remembered touching her. Running his finger around her mouth, then down her spine. God what an ass. Her skin. It was cold to the touch. He was sure of it. She was dying.

He sat back in his driver's seat and relived the last fifteen minutes. Her apartment door was unlocked, and he entered. Neve was in the living room standing by a small table, not dressed in much. A vixen if there ever was one. There wasn't much or any conversation. She knew what he wanted. He went over to her and grabbed her by the waist to kiss her. She put up a little fuss. She weaved, like her balance was off. Her eyes were half closed but he didn't put it together. He was more interested in her tied blouse that housed her luscious breasts. He undid the knot, rolled his tongue over her nipples, then, with his arm securely around her middle, guided her to the bedroom and dropped her on the bed. She sat like a wound-up doll…waiting. He played with her tits and when he let go, she slumped to her side. He peeled her thong down her thighs, then pushed her on her stomach. She didn't resist. She lay not uttering a sound. It didn't occur to him something was weird. He was too busy taking off his trousers. He slapped her ass, then parted her legs. It was only then…only then that it began to dawn on him something was terribly wrong. "Neve? You ready to put out? You do know how. I know you do." He touched her again. He called her a cunt. "What the fuck did you do?" He quickly grabbed his pants. He recalled screaming at her. Her face was pale, and her eyes slits. Jesus. He stood next to her, and a sick feeling washed over him. He had to get out.

Someone near his vehicle honked and he started. Sweat beaded on the sides of his face, although he was chilled. These kinds of things didn't happen to him. Control, he must seize the situation. He turned on his phone and lifted it toward him. The damn thing instantly went off and he nearly dropped it. Jesus Christ… Skinny, what the… He took a deep breath. The events of earlier in the afternoon came back to him. Nicole's office and who he believed had been there. His body warmed as the familiarity of command returned.

"Skinny, good of you to call. What did you find?"

"She's dead."

* * *

Whirley was seated not far from Jimbo. She didn't have to be obvious to spy. She was two or three tables in front of him. A perfect view of the waitress being very chatty. Whirley observed Jimbo's face, and although she couldn't hear the words all that well, moves were being made…any port in the storm. To think she felt a little guilty about screwing up Jimbo's life.

Whirley sipped the glass of water in front of her and got to thinking. There was no question what Jimbo had in mind, but what about the waitress. A one-night stand going for sexual fulfillment. Another notch on bagging an older man. She chuckled.

It wasn't difficult to get a man, any man; she was living proof. Or did the waitress believe her white knight had arrived to free her from her mundane life? Throw in love and loyalty, and sex gets all fucked up.

She could use some bread. She motioned for a waiter or waitress, anybody. The perky one finally left Jimbo. She didn't hide her smile well.

"What can I get you?" The nametag identified her as Annie.

Whirley almost blurted out something she'd regret, instead she asked for a scotch. "No, make it, bourbon on the rocks, and bread."

"Any particular…"

"Angel Envy and it better be a good pour."

Annie went toward the bar. Whirley viewed her tight jeans and rated her backside a six or seven. Jimbo would have a good time. In between her gazing and evaluating, a bus boy dropped the complimentary basket on the table. She snatched a slice and gobbled it down.

Annie's rear was nice but not as good as hers. But why the hell should she care. Somehow she felt competitive when there really wasn't a contest. A few minutes later, Annie returned with her drink. She plopped it on the table, mumbled, "Your drink, ma'am," and returned to Jimbo.

Ma'am? Did that little perky thing of a girl call me Ma'am? Damn. Whirley drank a finger of it. The stuff went down easy and smooth. A few more years and her time will come. *We'll see if little Annie's body can still lure, much less bag them…the little shit.*

Annie was ignoring her for her chance to score. What a dumb ass. She didn't have to work so hard to get him. Whirley knew that from experience. Jimbo wasn't exactly prime material. He'd do in a pinch but come on.

Jesus, if she didn't get some real food in her soon… She was out of bread. The temptation to do something mean was growing. Her stomach growled and time was wasting. There were other bars to hit. Sunday was a great time to get lucky…a lot of lonely men.

Then again, if she got a meal she could just go home and give Brandt a jingle. She emptied her drink.

Now if little Annie was fooling around with someone like Brandt, that'd be different. Of course, that would never happen. Brandt had taste and more restraint than Jimbo. Whirley played with her fork as she watched the pick-up dance between them. She sneered. She could write what was going to happen. Jimbo would fuck her brains out, then make an excuse he had work in the morning and duck out as fast as he could. There wasn't much there. She could warn her but little perky would never listen. Nor did Whirley at that age. Perky would have to learn on her own.

Whirley didn't want to make a scene, but she was famished. If it meant no food for her, then she'd add a twist to Jimbo's little night fling. She sucked down the last of her drink. Annie hadn't moved from Jimbo's table. That was it. Whirley dug out her phone from her purse. It was drop a dime time. Surprise! She knew her contact as Joe although she was aware he was called Skinny. She punched in the number. "Hello Joe, it's me, Whirley. I've got a tip for you."

Chapter Thirty-Nine

Hill's heart jumped. The phone was to his ear. Did he hear Skinny right? Who was dead? Neve? How would Skinny know that unless…unless the boss called? Jesus, his mobile had been off; he tightened his grip on his cell and squeezed his eyes shut for a second or two. "Who died?" Hill asked again.

"Lori."

"Lor… Wait a minute." Hill whipped his phone in front of his face and stared at the screen. He caught his breath. This was bad but he felt a weight lift. "Skinny, you said Lori was dead?"

"Yes sir."

How to play this? Did he want to know the circumstance or was it safer not to, particularly over the phone? Hill debated, tapping his fingers on the side of his cell. His curiosity got the best of him. "You found her that way?" His eyes narrowed waiting for the answer.

"No sir."

"Hmm." Not the response he was hoping. The obvious conclusion—Skinny fucked up. He knew it. The best thing was to stay calm and handle the situation step by step. "Where are you now?"

"Near her place. Cops were coming. I heard sirens."

"Get the hell out of there. When you're someplace safe, call me."

"Yes sir."

Hill pushed End. He wasn't a man who scared easily, but things were spiraling out of his grasp. He needed perspective and time to think. He couldn't sit in his car all night. He too had to leave, the sooner the better. But where? Return to the office? He was about to put his car in gear when his phone rang again. Now what? He glanced at the screen. The number was unfamiliar, but the area code was Chicago. Should he respond? Was it a hospital? Police? Jesus, the boss?

His mind flashed to Nicole in her office telling him about good work needs to be rewarded. He'd followed her advice and seized his moment, only instead of a piece of ass he was looking at an angry sea that could cost him his career. He had never been a religious man or held a belief in heaven or hell, but he sensed the world he knew was out of kilter. He balled up his free hand. He'd fight before he drowned.

He put his foot on the brake. "Yes?"

* * *

Everything was in a haze and distant. Voices and sounds seemed to come from inanimate objects. A pillow can't talk. Although, when Neve was a kid, all sorts of things did. In cartoons or Disney movies, anything was possible. Was she in one of those? A Neve in Wonderland? She heard herself laugh and float through the air. *Oh, my God I can fly. Ain't that something.* Look mom. Mom? Nicole? You're alive?

Mom waved. She was in a long coat, definitely had white gloves. It wasn't a hello gesture. "Mom, where are you going?"

Mom's mouth moved.

"What? Where are you going?"

Something held Neve back. She wanted to run after her mother. Was it someone's arm? A man? Daddy? Mom's image dissolved. Nicole?

"In here," she said.

Of course, it was her bedroom. Where else would she be. Nicole's hair was disheveled. Neve stood in the doorway and watched. "Who was your company? Didn't look like Jim. Was he nice? Was he good? Why?"

"Don't look sad, Neve, there's always room for you. You're my number one."

She didn't believe it…never believed it, but it was nice in the moment to be someone's first. She crawled into Nicole's bed. Nicole wrapped her arm around Neve and held her until Neve's eyes closed. She felt Nicole's hand caress her breasts. It felt so…

A nursery rhyme. Jack and Jill went up the hill…h-i-l-l, Mr. Hill, the sonofabitch. He slobbered over Jill's, mine? tits. He…? His breath was…sour. Oh, geez…did he fuck her, me? Oh, my God. Neve gasped. She was cold, then hot. She heard moaning. Was that her?

How did that rhyme go? Jack and Jill went up…

Jack and Jill went up…went up, what? Damn. Start again. *Jack and Jill went up ….*

The fuck'n hill…and…and… *took it home to mother dear.* That's it. *Who thanked her son and daughter. She thanked me. Mom thanked…me… daddy's little secret. Ssh.*

Nicole stroked Neve's hair and whispered her mantra, "It's all good."

The walls were a light beige, and there were people…two…maybe three… they repeated "Neve…" *How do they know my name?* She squinted. The ceiling light was bright. In the background there was a hiss of a machine. Why were these people masked? Her eyes opened a little wider. She noticed her arm hooked up to something.

"Neve, I'm Dr. Chevsky. You're in the ER at Northwestern Hospital."

"I am? Why? How?"

"A neighbor found you."

"A neighbor…?" Neve shut her eyes. "It's too bright. I think I'm going to puke."

"Keep your eyes closed. The nausea will pass. You overdosed on some antidepressants. The paramedics found several pills and open wine. You're reacting to the activated charcoal and bicarbonate we gave you to reduce the drugs absorption."

"Oh."

"We called your dad. He said he was on his way."

"Daddy? He's coming here?"

"Yes."

Her gambit worked. She took a chance and lived. Now, Daddy will take care of Mr. Hill. "That's good. That's…real good."

Chapter Forty

Detective Young pulled up to the late Lori Knight's home—a scene of controlled chaos— lights flashing, police cars from Chicago and Lincolnwood parked haphazardly, blocking street traffic, fire and ambulance trucks, and an evidence technician van. She parked a block away and walked through the police line. She saw Brandt standing on the deceased's driveway in a discussion with someone in plain clothes. She stood aside.

"This is a quiet neighborhood. Nothing happens on the block that someone doesn't see." The man explaining this was short and bald, older, dressed in a pair of khakis and a leather coat.

Young observed Brandt shift his weight, holding his notebook and pen to take down the man's information.

"Some guy earlier in the late afternoon came to Ms. Knight's door. He had a jacket with the company name written on the back…something like Smith or Jones Locksmith."

"Where were you when you saw this?"

"Oh, it wasn't me. The wife. She's the eyes of the block. She told me. Thought it was strange that a locksmith was there."

"Excuse me." Young joined the conversation. "Where did you say you and your wife live?"

The man pointed. "Those big bay windows let you see everything."

Brandt and Young glanced where the man indicated. The house was directly across the street.

"What time did your wife say this was?" Young continued.

"Not sure…maybe four or five."

"Can we talk to your wife?" Brandt asked.

"Sure, sure, she's sort of shy. Doesn't like confrontation and stuff. That's why she sent me. Anyway, the man went into the house, but she didn't see him leave."

"Can you or your wife describe the man?" Brandt asked.

The man waved his hand. "Hold on, I'm coming to the good stuff."

Young shot Brandt a look.

"The wife said that maybe a half hour to forty minutes later another guy was at their door. This time wearing a jean jacket. She couldn't see who answered, but she never saw either of the men leave."

"Did this second man have a different build than the first?" Young asked.

"Hmm, the little woman didn't say."

Young caught Brandt's eye, hiding their grins. "We need to talk to her. Mr.…?" Young took a step toward the man's home.

"Overbush, Myron and Ruth. Me and the wife been here fifty years. Saw Ms. Knight's house built. Let me think. She and her husband…Jim…I think that's his name, weren't the first owners. No siree."

"Let's talk to your wife, Mr. Overbush. We'll catch up on the history later." Brandt followed Young.

* * *

Skinny's hand shook while he kept the phone to his ear during his conversation with Mr. Hill. It wasn't like him to go off like he did. Damn the bitch for screaming. All he wanted was information. That's all she had to do. He pictured her when she answered her front door. She wasn't bad looking. Given the situation with her ex-lover boy, he may have… Jesus, broads on his mind at a time like this. The situation had gotten to him. Focus.

He had to get the hell out of there. He checked his sideview mirror. A car, two or three blocks down with lights flashing, was closing in. He pulled out with his lights off. As soon as he got to the corner he turned right. Sirens were getting louder. He flicked the switch for his head beams and drove several blocks before stopping to search his GPS for directions to the highway. He knew he should get out of the neighborhood. Mr. Hill expected him to. However, the strain of his afternoon labor made him hungry, and he could use a drink to steady himself. Besides, he'd be in better shape facing Mr. Hill with his belly full and his nerves settled.

He typed the word restaurant into his device, and it spit out the Edgebrook coffee shop and a little further toward the expressway was East of Edens. There's a name for you; maybe James Dean will be there. For the first time in a while, he laughed. *James Dean.*

Cop cars flew past him. He assessed the situation. That was a good thing. He didn't think anyone saw him enter Lori's or leave. He wore gloves, so no fingerprints. Did he forget anything? No, he was careful while there. Even the locksmith jacket was thrown away so if he was stopped, there was no connection. He relaxed a bit. He'd headed toward East of Edens. Not only did the name intrigue him, but it led him out of the immediate area.

The restaurant had a large parking lot and on a Sunday night there weren't many cars. He entered. There were two small tables in the entire place. At the counter, the man told him everything on the menu board was "to go." "Nobody eats here," he said.

Skinny glanced around and agreed. Not what he wanted, but what the hell. It was food and the car was as good a place as any. He ordered a gyros platter. So, he'd stink up his jalopy. It wasn't any great shakes to begin with. All the onions and stuff could make Mr. Hill keep his distance. Lord, would it come down to that? He shook his head. Jesus, what a mess.

He was out the door five minutes later with his meal. He put the white bag on the passenger seat, and set his phone on the dash. He carefully removed the food platter from the paper bag. Damn there was a lot of food—a real Greek feast. He poured the tzatziki sauce over the meat and loaded the pita with onions and tomato. He held the dripping sandwich with both hands, a napkin on his lap. The odor filled the car. He bit off a mouthful and enjoyed all the tastes and spices when his phone went off. *Oh shit, Mr. Hill?* He dropped his food onto the platter and swept his cell from the dash with one hand and used the napkin with the other. He quickly scanned the screen. He looked twice. Whirley? Now why…? He moved the platter closer to the passenger window. "Hey."

Chapter Forty-One

Hill said hello, then swallowed hard.

"Hill...?" ... silence.

Hill's hand tapped the side of the phone. It was always the wait. He was a master of it when he interrogated his prey. He'd watch as they squirmed although they'd try to hide it, but he knew. Silence was a weapon which he used well. Now he was on the other side. All he could do was imagine his fate. Where would the hammer land? He gripped his cell harder.

The voice at the other end began. It was tremulous, choked with emotion...JK. The reaction by his boss was unexpected and Hill took it as a small sign his universe may have steadied.

JK told him a doctor from the emergency room at Northwestern Hospital called. Hill held his breath. His mouth went dry.

"Neve overdosed," JK continued, his words tinged with disappointment, then anger. Hill heard the rattle of ice cubes when JK paused. The boss must be armed with his scotch.

Hill should have felt sympathy. The man poured his heart to him but for Hill, each tidbit of the telling brought elation. It was joy to the world. The bitch wasn't dead, and most importantly, her daddy would never believe a word of her story. Then JK hit him with another surprise.

"Get to the ER."

Wasn't irony sweet. She was his to do whatever he wanted. The boss had unknowingly written him a blank check.

JK's parting words called Neve a foolish girl, comparing his daughter to her mother. Then he uttered his bottom line:"Children aren't a blessing, Hill. They turn out ungrateful."

Hill nodded in agreement with a big smile on his face, although JK obviously couldn't see. He was still in charge and had nothing to worry about, at least from his encounter with Neve. Skinny was another matter. He'd take care of that.

* * *

"Whirley, what the hell are—"

She cut Skinny off. "Listen." Whirley put her hand around her phone and whispered, "I'm at a restaurant on Division Street. Jimbo is sitting a few tables from me going for the kill on a new squeeze. Just thought you'd be interested."

"Say that again."

"Jesus." She repeated her news.

"How long has he been there?" Skinny was doing a time calculation in his head.

"He was sitting at his table when I got here. Christ, what's the difference."

"Don't go over your skis, Whirley." Seconds later, he softened his tone. "You've been there for…"

"I didn't look at the clock, but I'd say at least twenty to thirty minutes. I still haven't seen any food."

"Stay hungry a little longer and I'll join you. He hasn't recognized you?"

"Are you kidding. He's so into scoring with the waitress he's not looking at anyone else. I also don't have long blonde hair. It's short and dark."

"Any other adjustments I should know?" He smiled. What he saw of Whirley the other night was okay by him…. more than all right. *Get with the program*, his inner voice intervened. He still had a small problem…Lori and Mr. Hill.

"I didn't think you noticed." She chuckled. "Everything that was, is still in place."

"Good to know. Give me the address, my boss would be very interested. Stay put but if he leaves, call. There will be something in it for you."

"Always ready to serve."

You bet you are, Skinny thought. He pressed End. He glanced at the passenger seat. The gyros had to go. He was no longer hungry…for food anyway. Whirley had given him, and for that matter Mr. Hill, an opportunity. Who better to have killed Lori… but the low-down cheating Jimbo. He figured Jimbo was the cops' numero uno suspect. He laughed. Life was funny…one minute the walls close in; the next, wide-open spaces.

He retrieved his gyros bag from the seat, got out of the car, and dumped the food in the garbage bin in the lot. He hurried back. Normally he'd call Mr. Hill and inform him of the latest development. But he understood Mr. Hill's aversion to discussing details over the phone. He'll handle this on his own. Give the cops the 411, then celebrate. Who better than with Whirley. An event Mr. Hill had already blessed.

Chapter Forty-Two

Ruth Overbush was a smallish woman, maybe 5'4" on a good day. She was seen in the alcove hugging the open front door. Her husband, Myron, led with Detectives Brandt and Young behind.

"Ruthie, dear, these officers want to talk to you about what you saw this afternoon," he said, standing just outside.

She motioned for her husband to come closer. "Didn't you tell them?" she whispered in his ear.

He nodded. "They want to hear it from you."

Her eyes widened and her face reddened. "Myron, I told you. I don't want to get involved." Her voice now a loud hiss.

"Are you worried about retribution?" Brandt jumped in.

The woman stared at Brandt, then took two steps farther into the house.

"Ruthie. Where are you going?" Her husband asked.

"It's okay, ma'am," Detective Young said in a soothing tone. "You won't be mentioned in any report. Your husband did a good job. There's a few things we'd like to know from you."

The woman stopped and gazed from her husband to the two strangers on the stoop of her house. "You won't mention our names...mine or Myron's?"

"That's right," Young said, motioning Brandt to put away his notebook and pen.

"Hmm..." She eyed Brandt and Young, then turned to Myron. "I'll receive those two in the living room."

Myron blocked the two officers from following. "It'll take her a minute or so."

"To do what?" Brandt asked.

The husband hunched his shoulders, a pain expression on his face. "My wife, she... well... eh... has a certain, you may say, peculiar way of dealing with people. Ruthie suffered a stroke some years back. Her entertainment is watching the goings-on of the street from that window I showed you. We don't get much company and when we do, she imagines herself as Royalty. Believe me I've been living with this far too long. But…" He raised his arms and sighed.

He turned towards the inner part of the house. "Are you ready, dear?"

"Yes. Show our guests in."

"This way." Myron did a short bow and with a flourish announced the two detectives.

Brandt and Young stepped past Myron and entered the living room. Ruthie sat on a high-back chair with the top of her head appearing from the cape wrapped around her.

"Do we curtsy and bow?" Young said out of the side of her mouth.

"How the hell do I know?" Brandt answered. A few seconds later, he tilted his head in a wayward salute and acknowledgement.

"Young man," Ruthie began, her voice strong and authoritative. "What is it you want?"

My God. She thinks she really is some sort of Ruler. What a whack job. This sure isn't taught in detective school. Well, I'll play along. "As the queen of this land," Brandt began, "your reputation is known far and wide for accurately reporting the goings-on of your kingdom."

Young bit her tongue. "What the f…?"

Brandt gave Young a sideway glance to shut her up. Then continued. "Did the first man you saw earlier this afternoon look different than the second?"

Ruthie lowered the cape so that her face was no longer covered. Her grayish tinged hair splattered across her head. "Other than the jacket, they seemed about the same in color and height. They were Caucasian. Both were large men in stature, and no, I had never seen them before or since."

"Your Excellency," Detective Young jumped in, "Did you see your neighbor Jim this afternoon?"

"I had other duties during a large part of the day. I had not gone to my royal balcony"—she pointed toward the windows—"until later in the afternoon."

The formality of the room was broken by a buzzing sound.

"What is that infernal noise?" Ruthie asked.

Brandt looked down. "Sorry, it's my phone. Excuse me." He hurried into the alcove by the door.

* * *

Whirley was running out of things to do while waiting for Joe. Watching the waitress carrying on with Jimbo was tiring. Being ignored was insulting. Jesus, time didn't move. She picked up her phone and went through her contacts. Brandt. What the hell. She dialed.

"Brandt, this is Carla. Sorry I missed you this morning."

"Carla—eh, I'm sort of busy at the moment."

"Yeah, I shouldn't have called. I know, bad of me. I'm a b-a-a-d girl."

"Are you drinking?"

"Hell yes. I'm at this restaurant on Division Street waiting for someone to take my order. There's only so much…hold on. There's still booze left in my glass."

Brandt heard a slurping sound.

"There's this guy a few tables from me. It's embarrassing. I know him. Anyway, Jimbo is falling all over himself trying to pick up this waitress. I'm bored, Brandt, waiting for this God damn…"

"Okay, I'm sure it's uncomfort… Look, I have to get back to this murder investigation."

"Murder! Wow. At least you're doing something. Okay, okay, I'm wasting your precious time. I got it. Hey, Brandt, let's get together soon. Makeup for lost time and all that shit."

"Yeah, good idea. I've got to get back. Don't do anything stupid."

"Me? Nah. Jimbo ain't worth it. Although he's going to be in for a big…" She started laughing. "Sorry, but Jimbo is about to get fucked but not the way he's thinking. I'm going to go. God, life's a bitch."

Brandt, while listening, split his concentration from the phone to the nut in the high-backed chair. The Queen said something about a chariot and a license plate number. He hoped Young paid attention. Straining for more detail, he absently pushed End on his mobile whether Carla was done or not. He took a step toward the living room, then stopped. "Jimbo?" Holy crap.

Detective Young took a few steps back from the crazy lady, and with her hand at her side hoped to signal Brandt to return from the alcove. The nutcake in her meandering of events recited a license plate number of a vehicle belonging to the person she claimed had been at Lori's door. Young whipped out her phone and typed in the information. *No shit did this queen of the block…Hell she rattled off numbers that sound real. Or maybe it was the mutterings of one not all there. Nonetheless, it was a lead.*

Mrs. Overbush stopped in mid-sentence. She stared at Young, wagging her index finger. Her voice turned shrill. "Are you recording me, young lady? I won't have that. None of that. Guards, grab her."

Young backpedaled toward Brandt and the front door. It was time to go. Out of nowhere the husband appeared, moving toward his wife. He put his arm around her shoulder.

"It's all right, Ruthie," his voice dripping with kindness. "Those people are leaving. You can go back to your Royal perch. It will only be a minute." He made a motion toward the door.

Mr. Overbush didn't have to ask twice. Young caught Brandt and gently shoved him outside.

"We have a lead," Young said to Brandt, pointing to her phone.

"Yeah, so do I. I know where Jim is."

Chapter Forty-Three

Neve lay on a gurney in her small cubicle of the emergency room listening to the beeps of the various machines connected to her. She followed their displays. Numbers appeared, disappeared, and re-appeared. As she breathed, a "3" flashed, then transformed into a "7" or a "9." Graphs showed the beat of her heart, then a readout of a number. It made no sense to her. Which was the better? A higher digit or lower? She didn't know what to root for. After a while she didn't care. She wanted to leave.

A social worker came by to discuss her mental health. She blabbed about the need for therapy, and that Neve had so much to look forward to. The worker should only know the crazy fucked-up world in which she lived.

Neve listened politely. What else could she do? The social worker scribbled a phone number on a pad of paper and told her to call when she was discharged. *Right.*

Neve watched her leave. It wasn't therapy she required. She needed. Yeah, needed was precisely the word. Neve moved her arms as best she could and hugged herself. Nicole appeared and replaced Neve's arms and held her. She caressed Neve's breasts and roamed over her body. She moved from Neve's chest to her stomach, to her thighs. This was what Neve craved and longed for. Neve looked into Nicole's eyes. They were mirthful, dancing, filled with excitement.

Nicole continued to play in her head. She heard Nicole's voice whisper in her sultry way, "Neve, you're the most important and precious thing on earth." She wanted to believe it was true. To have someone love Neve for Neve. If only…Nicole's whisper faded. Neve saw a man get up from Nicole's bed. She wasn't sure of the features but knew the scent… knew the aftershave…knew it well. It all crashed. Liar. Nicole was all lies. If only….all the screwed-up shit would go away. She reached for a Kleenex…Nicole, Hill, Jim, Charlie, and yes Daddy.

A nurse opened the curtain around Neve's hospital bed in the emergency room. "How you feeling? Your numbers just spiked."

Neve batted her eyes. "No. I'm okay…tired. I had a bad dream. Can I go?"

"You're a lucky girl. It was touch and go when they brought you here." The nurse scanned the various monitors and punched numbers into her iPad. She stuck a thermometer in Neve's mouth and grabbed her wrist. After a minute she let go, then examined the results of Neve's temperature.

"Well, you're normal, now. All of your numbers are good. I'm giving you this pamphlet about drugs and rehab. Look it over. Most of the kids who come in here like you toss it. Think it's garbage. Honey, be smart. It can save your life."

Neve eyed it. "Sure, no problem." She let it lie on the blanket. "So, I can leave?" she asked after the nurse let silence settle.

"Dr. Chevsky has to review your chart, then make that decision. He'll be along in a few minutes."

"Can I get dressed?"

"I'd wait, honey. You were one sick lady." The nurse parted the curtain and left.

The emergency room had its own rhythm. There was the humming of the typical sounds, of machines, doctors, nurses, moving at a non-hurried pace. Somber patients behind curtains presenting their pain and concern.

The swinging doors of the ER burst open. A new patient wheeled in. The tempo changed to a mad rush of humanity. Voices tense, shouting orders, bells went off, lights on a cubicle flashed red. Her sense of time blurred, and, in that chaos, a life passed or was saved. The clock ticked again. Time once again relevant.

There were no clocks that Neve could see. She was fidgety and the wait for the doctor, unnerving. She eyed the machines and had half a mind to disconnect herself. She moved her hand to do just that but stopped. Buzzers would go off. There would be no going home. She'd wait. Think about what she'd say to her daddy and what he'd say to her. His face would have disappointment all over it.

"Neve, how could you? After all I've given you." His voice commanding. No sympathy from him. When would she tell him? "Daddy, I've got something to tell you. Listen. Hill did this…"The curtain drew apart. The doctor entered.

Dr. Chevsky stepped into Neve's cubicle, his iPad in hand. He looked at her, a half-smile plastered on his face. He glanced at his screen, running his finger down a column. His demeanor serious.

"Well, doc, I'm okay. Aren't I?"

He hesitated, then spoke. "You are for right now. My concern, which also should be yours, is what happens tomorrow. You survived your overdose. If there's another one, you may not. Luck was with you."

"There won't be another one."

Chevsky studied her. "I hope for your sake. There are programs…"

"Yeah, the nurse told me."

"I hope you take advantage of them. They'll help you."

Neve looked around the room for her purse. "Is my father here?"

Chevsky looked down at his screen for a second. "Got it."

"Can you get my hairbrush? It should be in my bag. Daddy wouldn't be happy if I looked like shit."

The doctor grabbed the item from a chair next to the bed.

"Thanks, I've got to look presentable." She chuckled. "Or at least try. Daddy is particular…"

"A Mr. Hill is waiting for you outside the ER. I'll let him know when you're ready. After the nurse unplugs you, you can get dressed."

"What?" She held the brush to her hair. "My father isn't here?"

"No, he sent Mr. Hill. Is there a problem?"

She drew a breath and wiped her eyes to prevent a tear. "No…not a problem."

The doctor turned to leave.

She clenched her teeth, then relaxed. "Hey…Doctor Chevsky…thank you…"

Chapter Forty-Four

Jim gave Annie, his waitress, a long hard look as she went back to the kitchen area. Her shapely backside stood out. His luck was changing. Whatever will happen between him and Annie was… He was getting ahead of himself. He shouldn't even be thinking of being with her. It would only complicate things further. Wasn't there enough on his plate? He played with the spoon on his table, spinning it around.

He should call Lori again. Maybe whoever answered her phone was gone, or it was all a mistake. And Neve and Hill? Jesus, did Hill kill her? He stared blankly out the window. His mind refused to believe he witnessed a murder. Neve was breathing when he touched her, wasn't she? He wrapped his hand around his drink. He was losing his appetite.

His thoughts went back to Neve's apartment. Who was the woman who entered her place? Could that have been Charlie? What the hell was she doing there? He tilted his head and finished the last of his Johnny Walker. He swirled the remaining ice in the glass.

It was too much to worry about. *Calm, baby, it'll all work out.* If he happened to fuck Annie, that was all positive. He'd have a place to stay for the night. The morning would bring what it would. Right now, a warm bed and body next to him, along with another drink, would do him good.

He searched for Annie and noticed a woman a few tables away. Was she looking…staring? He glanced at her for a moment, then returned to hunting for Annie. As he scanned the restaurant, he snuck another peek. The woman's face bore a resemblance to… He must be out of his mind. Couldn't be. Her hair was dark and short, not blonde. It had to be the pressure of the last few days. What the hell would Whirley be doing here? Impossible.

Annie returned with his order, snapping his thoughts. She placed the plate of food in front of him.

"You want another?" She pointed to his empty glass.

"Yeah, that would be great. Long day…"

"You're sweet when you're embarrassed. I like that shy smile."

"Am I blushing?"

She laughed. "If you mean is your face turning red, no. Sort of pinkish."

The hell with Lori, Neve, and all the other troubles plaguing him. This babe wanted to jump out of her uniform to be with him. What a find. "When did you say your shift was over?"

A smile crept over Annie's face. She brushed aside some stray hair. She pointed to the man welcoming in the diners. "That's the boss. The place slows down after eleven. I'll talk to him." She grabbed a French fry from his plate. She threw her head back and had the long thin fry touch her lips and slowly disappear into her mouth. She righted herself. "I love them…crisp and salted just right."

His eyes widened as he watched. Ignoring the innuendo, he kept his voice steady. "If you say so." He tried one. "Yep, you're right."

She grabbed another fry. "Don't rush. I'll get you that drink."

He nodded, still wowed by her display. As Annie turned to leave, he caught a glimpse of that woman seated a few tables down. She was on the phone. Their gaze met.

* * *

Young was brought up short by Brandt's pronouncement. "You do? You know where Jim is?"

Brandt looked like the cat that swallowed the canary. "Yeah, eh, sort of."

Young looked back at the Overbushs' house. The crazy one stood by the bay window staring. Her mouth was going, and she

179

wagged her index finger toward them. "That bitch is giving me the creeps. Why don't we cross the street."

Brandt glanced at the Overbushs' window. "Sure. The queen must really be carrying on. How does her husband stand it? Poor guy." He followed Young to the other side. They stood by the curb and watched Lori's body being wheeled out of her house and loaded into the medical examiner's van.

"I never get used to that. Poor woman."

"So, you found Jim?" Young asked again, ignoring the tragedy of a life taken.

Brandt turned his attention away from Lori's gurney. "He's on Division Street at a restaurant."

"That narrows it. Which one?"

Brandt checked his phone. After several seconds he looked up. "Not sure, but my source would know."

"Source?"

Brandt shifted his weight. "It's really a friend. She called while we were… It doesn't matter. The bottom line is, I realized they're at the same place."

"Are you blushing?"

"I wouldn't know. We should get down there before he leaves."

Young held up her phone. "Before we rush off, the queen, as you called her, rattled off the license number of a van. She claimed it's of the person who came to Lori's door."

Brandt put his hands in his coat pockets and took a step. "Call it in. Maybe there's something there or not. You have to admit, Jim had every reason to kill Lori, and he had access. He lived with her."

Young let his words sink in. Her stomach tightened. Brandt may be right about Jim, but it wasn't Lori who was his victim, but Neve. Damn, why did she ever allow Nicole… Truth be told, Nicole only presented an opportunity. She went in with eyes and everything else wide open.

She watched Brandt waiting for some response. If he knew how deep she was in this mess. God. She must stay strong. She glanced at the Medical Examiner's van. How could she plant that jewelry in Lori's car and the underwear in Jim's. How evil was she?

The night before Nicole's death, she got a call from... She didn't know, couldn't tell whether it was male or female. Whoever it was used a voice distorter, claiming it was on behalf of JK, Neve's father. The speaker knew about her, Nicole, Jim, the whole mess. It was either do what was asked or...or be ruined. Hell. She made the choice. She used jewelry Nicole gave her as well as underwear. She should have thought, why, but she didn't...too scared...too selfish...too needy. Now Lori was dead and who knew if Neve had joined her.

She swallowed and momentarily passed her hand over her stomach.

"You doing okay? Brandt asked.

"Huh, oh, it's nothing. My stomach rumbles when it has food and when it doesn't. It has a mind of its own." *Jesus.* Brandt kept looking at her. *I can't say anything. Shit.* "Why don't you go in your car, and I'll catch up. When you find which restaurant, text me. I'll follow-up on the license plate."

"Hold on. You doubt Jim's the guy?"

"I..."

"Mother f... We have to be on the same page, Charlie. Jim's a bad dude. We can nab him."

"I get it, Brandt. I do." She put the collar of her coat up as the wind kicked from behind. She took a step closer. "We just spent time, a lot of time, with that...that woman across the street. The description she gave doesn't match Jim. Maybe she made it all up, in which case Jim is the primary suspect, but what if she didn't?" She held the screen of her cell toward Brandt." I need to check it out. You get the hell out of here and pinch Jim. I'll be a few minutes behind."

Chapter Forty-Five

Skinny hopped on the Edens Expressway to travel south to Division St. He shifted the mess he left at Lori's to the back of his mind. He felt giddy. No one saw him and no one knew him so the chance of being linked to her death was slim…better than slim…almost none, and with Jimbo about to take the fall. He pounded the steering wheel with his fist. He'd be in the clear. He was certain Mr. Hill would see it the same way.

He occasionally glanced at the speedometer. The needle hovered past sixty, but he wasn't thinking about that. Once Mr. Hill was satisfied, everything else… He had to think all this through. You never knew where one stood with Mr. Hill. The smile disappeared and he stroked his face.

Mr. Hill was a funny guy… not ha-ha funny, but strange, distant. He was not the type to have a beer with and chew the fat. Naw, he'd wear that damn coat of his no matter the weather even inside a bar. He'd let you blab on. His only reaction, no matter what was said, would be a stare that went through you.

Mr. Hill and the boss, JK, had been together for a long time. An unlikely pair if you'd asked him. J. K had personality, a back slapper with a roaring laugh who liked having a good time. Never knew exactly what he really thought, but what the hell… Mr. Hill…geez, was all business. Mr. Hill, though, was loyal. He'd do anything for JK.

Skinny smiled at that. Hell, he was the one who did the real dirty work. He took a deep breath and the slight queasiness he felt seconds before lifted. God damn his reward was waiting, and he'd be a fool not to take it after turning in Jimbo. It'd be Whirley's last dance. A shame to get rid of her, but that's what Mr. Hill ordered. That's what happens when you know too much.

Whirley had played a role in too many downfalls of up and comers whose ambition and sex drive got them in trouble. He drummed his fingers on the wheel. A momentary thought flashed by that he was following the same path, but he shook it off. He earned the opportunity. Mr. Hill said so himself.

He half closed his eyes imagining what it would be like to take her. He was feeling it. All the magic of her body, putting out just for him. What a scene. She lying naked…lost in the fantasy. He didn't see the taillights of the car in front. A few seconds late, that's all it took.

Shit…Whir…ley.

* * *

Detective Young watched Brandt drive away. She knew he was pissed that she wasn't totally on board with his theory. The hell with it. Brandt only got it half-right about Jim. She moved from the curb toward Lori's house and asked one of the beat officers, whose nametag read Sharritz, to use his on-board computer to check out the license plate number the crazy woman gave her. They walked over to his car. He got in, turned on the computer, and typed "JWP4796 Il." The letters and digits flashed on the screen.

"It sometimes takes a few minutes. Depends on how busy a night," Sharritz explained.

"No problem." Young leaned into the driver's window.

Nothing happened. The officer rebooted the machine and typed the information again.

"Funny, this never happens on television," Young said, eyeing her watch and wondering how close Brandt was to Division Street.

"This ain't TV, Detective. The city doesn't give us the latest in computer technology. This here must be close to seven years old. It takes its own sweet time…no matter your hurry."

"You got that right." She checked the hour again. "Listen, do me a favor. Call me on my cell when you get the information." She straightened. "Oh, and check if there's any warrants or criminal history when and if a name pops up. Here's my number."

"Got it, Detective."

Young half-jogged to her car and got in. She dropped her purse on the passenger side, then sat back in her seat. She grabbed another cigarette from her emergency pack and lit it. Her heart raced due to the pressure of all the cross-currents swirling in her life. She was learning firsthand buried secrets don't stay that way forever. Damn Nicole, damn Neve and Jim, and all the others. She placed her hand over her chest as if that would calm her heart. She knew what she must do. All that crap had to be pushed to the side. She had to find the strength and keep her wits about her. She inhaled deeply and when she exhaled, she regained a sense of calm. Her deeds were still unknown. Nicole was dead and couldn't talk, and Neve, if she was alive, wouldn't. For now, that left Jim, who knew of her but hadn't put it together. *Start the car*. She still had control. If Jim goes down for Lori and Neve, so be it. Silence—her savior.

Chapter Forty-Six

Neve sat up as Dr. Chevsky left. He had looked surprised by her thank-you, for maybe a half second. "You're welcome," he said and turned on his heel and closed the curtain. What the ... Who the hell was she to him, anyway? Another know-it-all child/adult, one of many who passed through—a rich spoiled one. The type who didn't appreciate what she had. Who was "lost," whose unhappiness was over having too much and not too little. She'd been accused of that many times. It did describe her and admittedly it was partially true. She had whatever she wanted except the one thing that couldn't be bought. It wasn't reflected in the numbers spit out by the machines attached to her. The doc couldn't read it on his iPad. No sense feeling sorry for herself. Those were the cards dealt.

Daddy isn't coming. Christ!

She made a big mistake with Nicole and let herself be carried away with Jim and Charlie and any college boy who came calling. It was fun to a point. She must have inherited Daddy's libido.

Show some T&A and if a woman had a certain look, Daddy would be there. Morals played no role, married or not on either's part, single, engaged, he would seize the opportunity.

Nicole was like that too, except in place of financial gifts, she offered love—not only sex but affection; endearments, security—at least to her. They were two of a kind, really, only their rewards were different. Who the hell was worse: Daddy or Nicole?

Daddy isn't coming. He sent his gofer, Mr. Hill, who must be hot to trot at having another chance at her. Jesus.

Daddy and Nicole...what a pair. If Nicole was alive, she wouldn't pick her up at the hospital, either. She, though, would at least make an excuse. She'd weave a heartfelt explanation, make it sound like it tore herself up inside, but, you know, she was "tied up"… and couldn't make it.

"Take care of yourself, honey," she'd say, "there's treats for you when you get home. I hope you'll be up for it."

Daddy did the same thing to Neve's mother—never visited or called when she was dying in some God-forsaken room in a shitty-ass hospital. His only show of mourning was to pay her funeral bill, not out of respect, but for appearances. It was always about how something looked.

Bitch, Bastard.

Daddy sending Hill. Coward.

She laid back on the gurney and waited for a nurse to unplug her.

* * *

"Excuse me, I'm here on behalf of Jason Kahn, Neve Kahn's father. I believe she was brought here by ambulance some hours ago. I've been instructed to take her home upon her discharge." Mr. Hill glanced at his watch.

The nurse at the desk checked her computer. There was a note by the patient's name stating the father's instructions. "I'll inform the doctor and patient you are here. Dr. Chevsky will be talking to her. When he is done, a nurse will disconnect her, then she'll get dressed. It'll take another twenty to thirty minutes depending how busy the staff is."

"That long." He looked at the time again. "I wouldn't think that there was that much to say."

The nurse eyed him coldly.

"Thank you. I have to make a call."

The doors to the entrance of the Emergency Room slid open as Hill stepped through. The little twerp overdosed, there was nothing more to it. A couple of hard knocks was all she needed to set her straight.

He soaked in the cold of the night. The chill turned his attention to his other issue…Skinny. He weighed the pros and cons of calling. Even if his phone records were obtained, he was where he was ordered to be. It would be normal procedure to check on his subordinate who claimed he had car trouble. He congratulated himself for conceiving the excuse. He only had to remember it. Hill grabbed his phone from his pocket and dialed. There was no answer. *Damn.* He stared at the screen for several seconds, then called again with the same results. More worry. Did the cops arrest him? He fought his emotions. It wouldn't be like Skinny. The man was too smart to let himself get caught. The last he heard, Skinny was about to drive away. *Shit, what if he didn't?* He felt beads of sweat form on his brow despite the cold. Should he call JK? He took a deep breath and discarded the idea as a panic move. He was in control. No sense jumping to a bad conclusion without more information. Time would sort things out. If Skinny was arrested, he'd call. That hadn't happened.

Hill returned to the waiting area of the Emergency Room. More than twenty minutes had passed according to the clock on the wall. He brightened at the thought of having Neve in his grasp. Skinny would have to wait. Rewards don't come often, and she…

He approached the nurse at the desk and asked again about Neve. She checked her computer, nodded. "The doctor discharged her. I'll see if she's ready."

"Thank you."

Hill adjusted his coat, then loosened his tie a bit. He eyed the door the nurse went through, then the clock. The waiting allowed his imagination to run. The scenario was evolving when the nurse's return interrupted the scene. Her face was flushed.

"I'm sorry, sir, she left."

Hill stared. His thoughts jumbled and it took a second or two for him to respond. "She's gone. Neve Kahn, the patient who came in because she overdosed, just walked out of here, even though you were told I was here to pick her up?"

The nurse's face paled. "Mr. Hill, she is over eighteen… and considered an adult. I'm sorry you had to wait, but we can't force her."

He drummed his fingers on her counter. "Do you know who her…. Never mind. You'll be hearing from us." Hill turned and raced out the door. He'd find the little shit. She wouldn't make a fool out of him. The only place she could be was her apartment. Neve was not all that smart or creative to be any other place. She will pay.

Chapter Forty-Seven

Brandt peeled out. His tires squealed as he drove off from Lori's crime scene. He was fuming over Young's half-hearted support. She violated the unwritten rule of policing: partners support each other. That's how a good department functions.

He went over the evidence again. Lori was found on the couch strangled. There was no forced entry or exit. No other fingerprints had been found, at least not yet. Jim obviously had access. He lived there. He had motive—Lori found out about his affairs. What was he missing? The crazy lady's description of another man at the door. How seriously could that be taken? She was nuts. That went for the alleged license plate too. Even if Young got a hit on the plate...so what? Mrs. Overbush could never testify. Never.

He eased up on the accelerator. He shouldn't be taking this so hard. It's another case in the long line of cases. He was going to flick on the radio but decided not to. He should take the time to clear his head.

He didn't like Jim, although that shouldn't be the reason to arrest his ass. The smirk and know-it-all-answers Jim gave when he was interviewed at the station the other night rubbed Brandt the wrong way. Jim gave up his affair with Nicole easily. He had no qualms admitting he was a cheating s.o.b. He'd fuck anything regardless of who got hurt. Brandt had no use for a guy like that.

Was he projecting? He shifted in his seat and concentrated on finding the entrance to the expressway. Once he merged with ongoing traffic, he continued his analysis.

He wasn't like Jim. Hey, every man was enticed by a piece, but that doesn't mean you grab it. He's been true to Carla although they had no agreement.

Hell, he understood what Young implied earlier this evening. Dinner? She wasn't talking about eating. What was her story? He couldn't put his finger on it, but she seemed different ever since they drove back from Nicole's and Neve's apartments. Was there some kind of connection between her and…one of them…Jim? He looked down at his speedometer for a second. Nah, preposterous.

* * *

Young's phone went off. She was a mile or two away from the crime scene, about to enter the expressway. "Yeah, Detective Young…"

"It's Sharritz. We got a hit on that license plate. The car was registered to a Joe Dinatto. His address is in Addison."

"That's quite a ride over to these parts. Any background?"

"Yeah. He's in the system. Most of it was little stuff, small time thefts, a few batteries, and some drugs. Fifteen years ago, though he did time for an armed robbery. In the last seven years he's been clean."

"How old?"

"Forties."

"What's the make of the vehicle?"

"Says here a twenty-fourteen Malibu."

"Chevy still makes those?"

"Guess so."

Young lit another cigarette. "Thanks, Sharritz, you've done good."

"Hold on Detective, there's one more thing. I reached out to Detective Brandt, but he didn't answer. The lab came back with a hit on a glass found in the bar sink."

"That was fast. Holy shit."

"I know. Detective Brandt must have lit a fire under someone's ass. The lab got a new machine—'the Ande'. It does rapid DNA technology."

"Okay." She rolled her eyes, impatient for him to get to the point.

"Anyway, they took a swab from the glass and compared it to those who have gone to the pen. Bingo. It came back to your boy…Joe Dinatto."

She almost slammed on the brakes. "Holy shit. I can't believe it. That crazy lady from across the street was spot on. Can you believe it?" She pounded the steering wheel. "Sonofabitch." She dumped the cigarette out the window. "I'll try Brandt. Jesus, will he be pissed."

She ended Sherritz's call. She was right—God damn it, Jim didn't kill Lori, but it didn't let him off the hook regarding Neve. What the hell was he doing in her apartment? Before she had a chance to think, she saw a sea of red brake lights and slowed her car to a stop. What the hell happened? It was late on a Sunday night, there shouldn't be much traffic. Sirens from speeding fire trucks, ambulances, and police cars in the emergency lane resolved the question. There was an accident somewhere on the road.

* * *

Whirley used her hand and phone to hide much of her face. Jimbo had caught her eye while sneaking another peek and there was a chance he recognized her. *Shit.* As soon as he looked away, she redialed Skinny. No answer. She checked the number on the display. It was Skinny's. *Now why the fuck doesn't he pick up? Not a nice way to treat a favor. Wasn't I helping him. Screw it.* If Skinny didn't care, Brandt did.

Whirley called Brandt. She looked away and waited for Brandt. Nothing. *Jesus.* What's with these guys? You hand them a gift on a platter—couldn't be easier. Damn them all. She tried again. She wasn't superstitious but perhaps it wasn't her night. She was wasting precious time if she was going to hookup with someone and make a few bucks. They couldn't expect her to hang around forever. Besides, she had a slight buzz thanks to the drink and no food. Either someone had to take her order, or it was time to go.

Annie breezed by Whirley's table again despite Whirley raising her hand for attention. Her false smile quickly disappeared as Annie made a bee line to, Whirley guessed, the boss. The conversation appeared a bit animated but didn't last long. Whatever was said between the two, Whirley didn't wait to find out. She slipped out the door figuring the house owed her the drink.

* * *

Jim was often accused by Lori of not being a detail kind of guy. It was one of her big complaints. He'd conceded it was true, but not when it came to women. On that subject, if he was attracted to someone, he'd remember. The eyes of the lady sitting a few tables from him had promised a sexual feast the night before. It was hard to forget, either. Her hair was different, but not the face or the body. That was Whirley, pretending not to see. *Crap*. He nudged his plate of food a little to the side and left his hand on top of the bun. Was this coincidence?

He searched the room for the guy who took the pictures of them. He didn't appear to be there. Small consolation. Jim didn't need to be reminded of what happened the other night. The bastard popped out of somewhere. He worried about the symmetry if the picture guy was about to do it again. At least this time he was dressed, and no bitch had her mouth near his dick.

His hand shook a little when he went for his glass of water. Whirley was screwing with him again. He had an almost sure thing with the waitress. How could he be so cursed? He had to leave. Who knows what Whirley had planned? Given his circumstance, he couldn't take the chance. He had to figure another plan. Neve, G-d Neve, she was out, hopefully alive, but… He'd give Lori another call. He'll patch it up with her. He could play at being contrite. He'd done it before.

Jim grabbed his phone and dialed. He listened to the beeps. He pictured Lori when they first met, the first kiss, the first time they went to…

"Hello." It was a male voice.

"Hel… Who's this? I'd like to speak to Lori."

Jim heard several voices in the background. *What the hell was happening?* "Hello," Jim raised his tone.

Someone with a very deep voice responded. "Sergeant Halleck, here. Who's calling?"

"Serg—? … police? What's going on?"

"Who is this?"

"I'm a…a…friend. Lori's friend. Did something happen?" He squeezed the side of his phone. He heard the wail of a siren through the connection.

Halleck asked again for Jim to identify himself.

Jim hit End and stared into space. Seconds later, Annie tapped his shoulder. He jumped. His phone almost dropped from his hand.

"Something wrong? You haven't touched your food."

Jim did a quick scan of the dining area before answering. Whirley wasn't there. Was she gone?

Jim swallowed hard. "No, everything is okay. Really. Sorry, I was in some deep thought and didn't see you coming." He smiled warmly as he looked at her.

"Great. The boss said I can leave. I'll wrap the food if you want."

"That's okay. I wasn't all that hungry after all."

Her eyes lit up. "I'm sure we can find a way to remedy that."

Jesus. There was no mistaking the implication. "Okay then. What did you tell him?" He gestured towards the manager.

A little dimple brightened her face along with a mischievous smile. "Women issues," she said with a soft laugh. "Don't worry though, they'll pass quickly. I'll leave first and meet you at the corner."

Jim nodded. He watched Annie head toward the door. As soon as she was out, he stood, and visually scanned the restaurant. No Whirley, no camera guy. He walked briskly toward the front. Lori came to mind. The just-ended phone call to her flashed by. What was all that shit about? The best he could contemplate was an accident. Hopefully she wasn't hurt or injured too badly. He promised himself to check other later. For the moment, Whirley and the camera fiend were the danger. His safety was his prime concern. If that also included bedding his new-found friend, so be it. He got to the door without being stopped. He took one more look before stepping outside. What he cursed moments before was actually disguised as luck.

Chapter Forty-Eight

Brandt rushed out of his vehicle after parking on Burton between State and Dearborn. It was the closest he could get to Division Street. He checked the time. Forty minutes, give or take, had elapsed since first talking to Carla. He hoped he wasn't too late. All the arguments whether Jim did or didn't strangle Lori no longer mattered. He would find out for himself. He walked quickly without attracting undue attention to the corner of Division and State. Once there, he reached into his pants pocket for his phone. It wasn't there. He tried his coat. Damn, he must have left it in his car. *I'm an idiot,* he thought. Should have phoned Carla while on the way as well.

He stood next to the light pole on the corner, and viewed the many restaurants and bars lined on both sides of Division Street. Going into each would be hopeless. His shoulders sagged. All this time and energy spent, and he blew it. All because he was in a hurry and angry at Young for doubting him. Then again, where the hell was Young. She was supposed to be right behind him. She was his backup. He patted his pockets again. No phone. He knew he should return to the car. He didn't move. Like a gambler on a losing streak, he held onto hope that luck would swing his way. Maybe he'd spot Carla.

He eyed the street traffic. Clumps of people passed him while others went in and out of the various establishments. He wished he had a cigarette, although it wasn't cool anymore. Not for smoking, but to have something to do with his hands. He lost track of time. Was it two minutes or five? Hard to tell without looking at his watch. Doing so, though, would further drive home the point of the stupidity of his piss-poor plan. Even if he saw Jim, he had no backup, no radio, not even a phone. What a great cop and detective.

A woman caught his eye exiting a bistro five or six doors down. He noticed she appeared to be wearing only a sweater…not exactly appropriate for this weather. He stuffed that thought to the back of his mind and shifted his attention. If he had any chance of nabbing Jim, he had to get his phone. He took a step or two in the direction of his car, but, out of habit, gave the street another glance. The same woman was coming toward him. Her pace was slow—advancing a step, then looking over her shoulder. Brandt stopped. The street and car lights lit her face. She looked vaguely familiar as she drew closer. Had he busted her or had she been a victim of some crime? Time ran out for the answer.

She was a step in front of him. "Hey, Detective?" She stared into his face. "Oh yeah… it's Brandt."

He studied her. She looked young…perhaps late teens early twenties. "Do I…"

She did a quick glance over her shoulder. "You should, but what the hell. You probably never expected to see me again. Just another dumb broad sent up the river…so to speak. You should never, never had done that. The internet and the boy who got his comeuppance. A girl can only take so much." She glanced down for a second or two. "I was saving this for my new love who'll be coming in a minute or two. A good surprise is always worth it. Right, Detective?" She held his gaze.

He had focused on her face and hadn't looked. He didn't see her hand, her purse. "I know—" He saw the flash and smoke, immediately followed by the bang from the gun. He crumpled to his knees, then fell on his side. There were screams; he saw legs. Drawing breath became difficult. Peoples' voices all blended. He fought to keep his eyes open, but he was losing. Someone yelled or said something. Was it a question? What did they want to know… Annie…Travers…juvenile… murder. He took one more breath.

* * *

Jim heard a pop as he stepped outside. At first, he thought someone set off a firecracker. He looked in the direction of the sound, which came from the corner. He heard screams and as he got near, shouts. He saw two men run after someone down the street. He drew closer and witnessed one of the persons running tackle the one who was chased. At the corner, Jim saw through the still sparse crowd a male lying on the sidewalk. He made his way closer to the body. Seconds later his jaw dropped when he recognized the person the two men dragged back to the scene.

"We'll hold her for the cops." The man looked around. "Someone called, yes?"

Another answered, "Yeah. They're on their way."

Jim, his mouth dry, his heart pumping, spoke. "Annie?"

"You know this woman?" The tackler asked.

Jim shrugged, then took a deep breath. "No…no… not really. She was my…a waitress." He pointed to the bistro down the street.

There was a bruise on Annie's face, but she managed to smile. "Just a waitress…huh. We were going to be lovers. You remember, asshole? We were going to fuck like bunnies. Then I was going to give you the last best orgasm you ever will have. Fortunately for you, I bumped into the sonofabitch lying on the sidewalk."

Jim followed Annie's gaze and recognized the victim on the ground. "Holy shit. That's… that's a cop." Shocked. He stood frozen, drained. He couldn't find enough air to speak, but mouthed, *Why?*

Annie sneered and attempted to lunge but was held back. "The sonofabitch took years from me. Took me from my family and locked me in a hellhole for something I had a right to do. Payback time."

Jim heard the distant wail of sirens. He stepped back, hoping to fade into a larger group that had gathered.

"Hey, Mac, where you going?" one of the Annie's captors asked.

Jim didn't answer. Between the crowd pushing forward and the frenzy of arriving police and ambulances, he disappeared.

* * *

Whirley, once outside the bistro, called Skinny as well as Brandt without success. The hell with it all, she thought, and crossed the street to the other side of Division. Seconds later, Annie came flying out the restaurant's door heading toward the corner of Division and State. Did the little tart plan this with Jimbo? Whirley didn't take her eyes off her. So far, Whirley thought she was right as Annie kept looking over her shoulder as she approached the corner. Then things became weird. Steps from the perceived destination, Annie appeared to engage a man in conversation. *What the hell is Annie doing? Setting up a ménage à trois?* It being night, the buses and cars interfered with Whirley getting a clear view of the person. The next thing she heard was a loud pop, like a car backfiring. Whirley put her hand to her mouth. What the hell...Annie? Holy shit. Whirley spotted the person lying on the ground. She heard shouts of "Stop!" Three people ran diagonally across Division. Whirley saw two men chasing, Jesus Christ—Annie. It was over quickly. Annie was brought back to the scene.

A crowd formed. There, making his appearance, was Jimbo edging himself near the body. Whirley crossed the street. There were several people between her, Jimbo, and the victim. She heard sirens. The corner then exploded with blue and red flashing lights. She moved closer. Cops were jumping out of their vehicles. She was about an arm's length from Jimbo. She could have grabbed him. Instead, she glanced down. Brandt. A shiver went through her. *Oh, my God.* She looked wildly around. Cops surrounded Annie and her captors. She noticed Jimbo creeping into the bosom of the crowd.

None of this made sense. The whys, the could-haves, Jesus, Brandt was a good man. At least as good a person as any that passed through her life. Why would Annie, if that was her name, do... Tears welled up. Crazy to cry over someone she knew but not really. Would there have been a future with him? In her heart she knew…but…

The police pushed the crowd away from the deceased. "Move back," she was told. The press of humanity pushed her several steps off the corner. She didn't see Annie but caught the body being loaded into a van. It unnerved her to see Brandt that way. His features covered, his name exchanged for a number to be forgotten. She swallowed hard and forced herself not to cry. Unanswered questions rumbled in her mind. Why? What did Jimbo have to do with it? She couldn't go home and forget. She checked the spot where Jimbo had been. The sniveling bastard used the crowd to escape. She wasn't going to make it easy for him. She'd take it upon herself to hunt him down.

Chapter Forty-Nine

Neve examined the clothes the hospital staff left her. It wasn't her usual designer label wear, but considering she was rushed to the hospital with nothing but... a thong? Jesus, Hill, her apartment, the memory of his hands groping her, all returned. It left her sick. She shut her eyes tight, then opened them. Her little hospital room hadn't changed. The curtain was still drawn. There was a chair near her gurney, but the insidious noises from the various machines had stopped. There was no more chirping or beeping close at hand. No graphs and numbers flashing.

She swung her legs off the bed. It felt good not to be hooked to anything. She rubbed her wrist over the bandage the nurse provided. One of the reminders of the night. She quickly donned the sweatshirt, pants, and sandals provided. Dressed, she stood in the middle of the room figuring her next move. She had to slip away. She peeked out from the side of the curtain. On a chair in front of one of the computers, several feet from her, someone had left their white medical coat hanging from the back. That was her ticket. She walked from her cubicle, grabbed the coat, and put it on. The embroidered name labeled her as Dr. Susan Claire. Good enough. Instead of the exit to the emergency room waiting area, she took another door that went into the hospital. No one stopped her. The coat was her shield. She walked to the main entrance and stepped outside. The cold air never felt so good. She asked the attendant for a cab. A minute or two later, one rolled up.

"Where to, Doc?"

Neve shut the passenger door. "Uh," then gave the cabbie her home address. Where else could she go? All she had with her was a small purse and a credit card. Who got that for her, she didn't know, but was thankful. She needed cash if she was going to hide, and that was in her apartment. Anything else could be traced. She'd have to chance it and pray she could pull it off before Hill realized she had vanished.

Chapter Fifty

A sea of red taillights stretched in front of Young. It was mesmerizing and frustrating. She agreed to be Brandt's backup. More importantly, she had to stop him from arresting Jim for the wrong crime.

The damn traffic played on her anxieties. She had to keep Brandt close. All she needed was for him to suspect that she was involved with Nicole or God forbid Neve and by way—Jim. Everything she had worked for…gone.

Brandt must be using every four-letter word he could think of to describe her for not having shown up. That could explain why he hadn't answered his phone. Pique. Men weren't supposed to act that way. It was one of those nonsense descriptions of women. C'est la vie, as the French said.

She inched forward, the clock adding numerous minutes to the drive. She turned on the radio searching for a traffic update. After one advertisement after another, the announcer raced through the various expressways dropping a tidbit that there was a three-car accident on the Kennedy near Belmont with a fatality. G-r-e-a-t. With nothing else to do, she tried Brandt again. No answer. Christ, he's taking his pissed-offness a little far. Cars moved another foot or so. *What the hell.* She'll call Sharritz. After three rings, she made a connection.

"Sharritz? Detective Young again. I'm in my personal vehicle trying to meet Brandt but there's an accident on the Kennedy. Do you have any info on it?"

"Hey, Detective, I was just going to call you."

"You were?"

"Yeah, I have some news not totally confirmed, but it's grim."

"What?"

"There's an accident on the Kennedy."

"I know that. I'm in it."

"Sorry. The car with the fatality is our guy."

"Say that again. You sure?" Young gripped the phone tighter. A shiver went through her. Karma?

"The plate is the same and the guys at the scene found his ID."

"My Lord, this case is moving fast. Unbelievable. I'm going to try to get over there." She took her foot off the brake and moved a few feet. "Have you heard from Brandt?"

"No. I tried to raise him several times."

She tapped her fingers on the side of the phone. Strange even for Brandt. She wondered if something happened. "Well, keep trying. If you reach him, give me a jingle."

"Will do. Good luck."

Young checked her mirrors and flashed her headlights, steering her car to the emergency lane. It was slow but she made headway, reaching the accident.

* * *

"Hey, what the hell you doing? This is an accident scene." A burly cop with the nametag Killard slapped the side of Young's vehicle as it came to a stop.

Young flashed her ID and badge by the driver's window, then opened her door.

Killard stayed in front as Young stepped out. "Can I see your ID again?"

"Sure." She handed him her badge and wallet. "The victim of the accident may be involved in a homicide that happened a few hours ago. My shift was over, but when I heard the news, I decided…what the hell…being in the neighborhood, sort of to speak."

He quickly viewed Young's ID. "Well, you won't get a statement from him, Detective. He's dead."

"A shame. Besides his wallet, did you find anything else?"

Killard returned Young's IDs. "That's above my pay grade. I just protect the scene." He pointed to another officer standing by a wrecked vehicle. "That's the man to talk to, Sergeant Williams. Watch your step, though. There's lots of debris."

Young walked over careful to avoid stepping on scattered glass and automobile parts. She called out to the sergeant and introduced herself.

Williams had his phone to his ear. "I'm sort of busy, Detective. We have a fatality and several badly injured people." He pointed to the two other vehicles.

"I won't take much of your time. How did it happen?"

Williams lowered the phone. "A thumbnail sketch. The first car, here whose frontend is demolished, struck that Ford over there, who hit the Toyota now being towed."

"Got it."

Williams shouted an order to one of the ambulance drivers, then returned to Young. "What brings you here? This is traffic?"

"Yeah, I know, but the driver of the first vehicle, Joe Dinatto, seems to have been involved in a homicide that happened a few hours ago."

"No shit."

Young smiled. "Yeah, sometimes cases are all wrapped up in a nice bow. Did you find anything else?"

Williams stepped towards the demolished vehicle. "He had a phone on him. We haven't inventoried the contents of the car. There was a jacket in what was the back seat."

"Can I see the cell?"

Williams raised his eyebrows. "Detective, you know if you touch that evidence, I'll have to put you on paper. Then you'll have to make a supplemental report."

Young was about to respond when her phone went off. She retrieved her cell from her jacket pocket and recognized the number. "Excuse me, Sergeant. I have to take this." She stepped away, then answered, "Young here, what you got, Sharritz?"

"I'm afraid it's not good."

"Whatcha mean?"

"There was a shooting on Division and State. Brandt's dead."

The air seemed to have been sucked out of her. "No…no…no…it can't be," she gasped. "I…eh…how…did…it…happen?" She fought back tears. She walked around not paying attention to where.

"Hey, Detective, watch it," Williams shouted.

Young reacted in time to avoid an oncoming vehicle. Her hand shook and without thinking disconnected the call. Williams was a few feet from her.

"Everything okay?" he asked.

She drew a deep breath, then exhaled. "Yeah, it's all good." She returned her phone to her pocket. "Thanks for your time, Sergeant, much appreciated. Got to get going. My partner needs me."

"Sure thing." He walked back to where an emergency crew was huddled.

Young calmed as the cold air nipped her face. She got in her vehicle, rested her arms on the steering wheel, and sat watching but not focused on the world outside. She felt an emptiness, and for the moment, a loss. She was sorry for Brandt and herself. He was a good partner.

She searched her console for her stash of cigarettes. There was one left. *What the hell. It was one more occasion to savor.* She lit up and drew deeply. She did enjoy it, despite all the cancer bullshit warnings. It would have been fun to have known Brandt better. What was he really like out of uniform. That's fate—too bad. She took another puff and stared at the growing ash. A smile curved her lips. It wasn't for picturing him naked and experiencing the pleasure she may have brought. Although, that did cross her mind. No, it was the realization her secret was safe…very safe. She was amazed as to how jaded she'd become. This job of being a cop colored what was right or wrong. It was Brandt, wise and steady, who always reminded her to "cover her butt." She was now covered and covered well.

Chapter Fifty-One

Hill couldn't believe the amount of traffic on State Street heading toward Division. At the most, it was a twenty-minute drive to Neve's place. Not tonight. All day long his luck was in the toilet. From chasing that bitch in the office building, Lori, to Skinny, to… He sighed. Skinny. *Where the hell is that prick?* He hit the Call button on his steering wheel and told the device to call. The phone rang several times. He was about to switch off when a connection was made.

"Hello, Skinny?"

"This is Sergeant Williams, Chicago Police."

"Sergeant… police? Where's Joe?" Hill checked the number on the car's screen—*right number… wrong Goddamn person. Hard to believe Skinny got himself arrested.*

"Who's calling?"

"His boss. He told me he had car issues."

There was a pause. "What kind of problems, Mr…?"

"Hill." He had to think. "Well, Joe had been complaining he was putting too much money into the vehicle. He owned an older model… and guess he wanted some advice." Hill sensed Skinny was in deep shit.

"Well, Mr. Hill, your employee is deceased. He may also be involved in a…"

"Skinny—dead? "How…what happened?"

"A car accident."

"Holy shit, I mean…sorry, officer. I can't believe it."

"Understandable. We need to contact his next of kin. Do you have any such information?"

Hill shifted in his seat. "Off hand, I don't. I'll need to contact Human Resources. Obviously, they're closed. Text me your number and I'll get you that information in the morning."

"Will do. Mr. Hill, regarding the other matter…"

"What other matter?"

"Homicide."

The cars behind Hill blew their horns. He was so wrapped up he had forgotten to move. He checked his mirrors, swore silently, and stepped on the gas. "Did I hear you right?"

"Yes sir, you did."

"I have no idea. Skinny, I mean Joe, called me earlier, out of the blue, said he was having issues with his car. Didn't really listen to what those were. Said he should get a new one and I'd get back to him. In reading the paper this afternoon, I came across an interesting deal."

"You don't remember what kind of problems he was having?"

Hill sighed. "Really, I…I don't recall. He had a beater, any number of things had been worked on. Why Joe kept it as long as he did is beyond me.

"Uh-huh. What company did he and you work for?"

Hill gave him the name.

"Thank you, Mr. Hill. I'm going to pass this information to the detective working on that case. They'll probably reach out to you tomorrow. Is the number on the screen a good one for you?"

"Yes. It's my personal cell number."

"Very good, Mr. Hill. Sorry about Mr. Dinatto."

"Yes…you're most kind." Hill pushed End.

He drove about a block farther and pulled over. He realized his conversation with Sgt. Williams did not go well. He left himself open. *Car issues. Shit, any good dick could blow through that excuse with a bicycle. What the hell is the matter with me?* He knew better and was trained better. He was a chump all because of… He hated to admit it, but he had to be honest with himself—Neve. He rationalized it wasn't only the sex, although if he leveled, it was a part of it. The larger issue was she made a fool out of him and, though not likely, it could cost him…perhaps his job. The good thing, he still had control. All he had to do was find the bitch, teach her a lesson, then inform JK of the situation regarding his wayward daughter and Skinny. All doable unless emotions fouled up the plan.

* * *

The old lyrics of *Where you going to run to…ol' sinner man…* played in Jim's head. He knew one thing: he had to get far away from State and Division. He couldn't afford any more calamities. His pace was fast but not enough to draw attention. He went by Goethe on his way to Schiller, remaining on State. He had covered about three-and-a-half blocks. Police cars continued to fly down the street. He slowed as they passed, then turned to look behind him. The corner of the murder was lit up like the 4th of July.

Jesus, Annie shot a cop…a detective, no less. Why? He turned right on Schiller. *It could have been me. That's what the crazy bitch said.* She would fuck him, then shoot him. He stopped for a moment and wiped his face. Lady Luck was still perched on his shoulder.

He looked down the street. Neve's place was about a half block away. He drew his wallet from his pocket. Not much there—about seventy-five bucks. Not enough for even a closet in any of the hotels in the area. He moved away from the streetlights. Neve was either at the morgue or a hospital. Either way, her apartment would be empty. He hadn't locked the backdoor when he made his escape hours ago. He figured she had cash hidden somewhere. *What the hell.* She offered the money when she threw him out. He'd pay her back if she was still alive, and if she wasn't…

Jesus, it was like the old days when he'd be summoned to Nicole's apartment. Nicole's light on the third floor would be on, signaling he'd better get his ass up there. How did it all get screwed up?

He checked the street for anything unusual; no police cars, at least that he could tell. He doubted Hill or anyone else like Charlie would return to Neve's apartment. He ran his hand over his face and trusted he was right.

He ducked out of the shadows and started for the alley. He took three steps, then someone grabbed his shoulder. Startled, he turned. "Whirley, is that you?"

Chapter Fifty-Two

Young's phone rang, jolting her out of her reverie. She fished it from her pocket and while punching the Answer button, realized the caller number was unfamiliar. Too late.

"Hello, Detective Young? This is Sergeant Williams."

Young looked through the front window of her car, but the emergency vehicles hid Williams from view. "Hi. I'm in my car...haven't moved." She waved but doubted he saw.

"You're here?"

"You want me to come to you?"

"That's all right. I think I see the vehicle, now. I'll be right over."

Young got out and stood on the passenger side, the lit cigarette clutched in her right hand. Williams went up to her.

"I thought you left to help your partner."

Young stared off into the distance, then brought the cigarette to her lips. "Nasty habit." She took a puff. "The phone call I got was news that my partner's been shot. I was sitting in my car collecting myself." She walked a few steps, flicked the growing ash, and took another pull.

"I'm so sorry. I...eh..." He cleared his throat. "This may have something to do with your case...I don't know. If you'd rather go home and..."

"No." She dropped the cigarette to the ground. "What is it?"

"I got a call...actually the dead guy, Dinatto, got the call from his boss, Hill, minutes ago."

The mention of that name got Young's attention. "You said Hill?"

"That's right. He gave me the name of the company they both worked for and his cell number. Said that Dinatto had car problems."

Young didn't listen to that part. She recognized the company's name and had a growing realization of Hill's role.

"Get Dinatto's cell to the evidence boys and order them to do a search of the incoming and outgoing calls, right away. Sergeant, you did good…real good." She walked to the back of her car to get to the driver's side.

"Where are you going?"

"Division and State. That's where my partner was shot."

* * *

Neve was inside her apartment. She grabbed a bundle of cash courtesy of her part-time entrepreneurial salesmanship of "pharmaceuticals" and the occasional "service" provided to wealthy college boys. As her daddy stressed, nothing was for nothing. She counted out the hundreds until it added up to three thousand. It would keep her for a while. She returned the balance inside the shoe box hidden in the rear of her closet underneath a carefully staged pile of winter clothing.

She went about her planned escape methodically even though her heart pounded. The least unexpected noise made her jump. She left her room without touching anything else. She didn't want to mess with any DNA of Hill's that could be discovered. She crossed into her living room and approached the hallway to the door. She had left it open a crack. She heard the buzz of the call button for the elevator. She gasped. It wasn't difficult to figure whoever summoned that rickety old thing wasn't going to the third floor for Nicole. Her adrenalin began to pump, and she was ready to run out the door, but to where? She looked around her darkened apartment. She had a few minutes on whoever was downstairs. She raced to the dining room where she kept Nicole's key. She snatched the key out of the drawer and was about to shut it when the corner of a plastic bag caught her eye. It was the evidence bag with the snifter, she took from Nicole's apartment. *Who knows?* She seized it, dropped it in her purse, then closed the drawer. She crept as quietly as she could to her front door and listened. The elevator was still clanking its way down. She bit her bottom lip and took a deep breath. For a second, she thought maybe it was Daddy. *Couldn't be. It isn't his style. There's nothing in this building for him.* She swallowed. *The dirty bastard.* It had to be Hill down there. No one else knew she was out of the hospital. No one else had a score to settle. She closed her door quietly and took the stairs. The elevator was now clamoring up. Her hands shook a little as she unlocked Nicole's door. Before closing it, she listened and heard knocking on the floor below. First it seemed polite, then it got louder. She didn't need to hear more. She shut the door quietly, then used the sliding chains to lock it. With her back resting against the door, Neve whipped out her phone. She sent a text to the only person she could think of who could help. *Charlie, come quick. Hill—*

Heavy footsteps.

Chapter Fifty-Three

Sinclair Watson owned the first-floor apartment in Neve's building. Earlier that Sunday evening, must have been sometime after seven closer to eight, he had settled himself into his easy chair with a glass of cognac and waited for the basketball game to begin. Someone pounded on his door. Scared the hell out of him. His wife from the kitchen asked if he heard the doorbell ring, then knocking. He wasn't deaf.

"It's probably nothing," he said and consoled himself this wasn't the first time such a thing happened. Ever since Nicole and later Neve moved in, a peaceful night was a challenge. So many times, his sleep, but not his wife's, had been interrupted due to the clanging of the elevator by Nicole's guests as well as their wild laughter ricocheting through the building.

The knocking persisted.

"You better answer," his wife ordered.

Sinclair glared at the TV as well as the delicious glass of amber-colored Eau de Dieu, mumbled to himself, and went toward the front entrance. He stopped in his tracks when he heard a female voice scream, "Call nine-one-one!"

"Did you hear that?" his wife asked.

Of course, he did. He was on high alert as he opened the door. "Hello?" He searched the hallway but didn't see a soul.

"Who was there?"

"No one." Sinclair closed the door and headed back to his chair. "Damn kids."

"We better check on Neve." His wife insisted.

"What?... Why?"

He waited for her answer. Ever since Nicole, then Neve moved in, there had been a lot of coming and goings. It got so, he'd leave his bed and peek out his door. It was better than counting sheep.

The men and women partied to all hours of the night. They were young, as he once was. It was like reliving a lifetime ago.

"We're neighbors," she said, "and whoever that woman was sounded hysterical."

"Yeah?" He knew it was useless to argue. He had one failed marriage, years ago. But he was different then; drinking and carousing seemed to be the thing to do. Now, he and his wife settled into the upper middle-class lifestyle, shopping Michigan Avenue and dining at the latest places.

"I'll go." He'd never hear the end of it if he didn't. He trudged up the stairs to Neve's apartment. Strange, her door was open. Nicole would do that too, on occasion.

It was about a month before the night Nicole died, Sinclair caught an older man before daylight making his way to and, several times, from Nicole's apartment. Given Nicole's beauty and age, Sinclair understood, but had to smile. Life had taught him it wasn't necessarily for the man's prowess. It was more likely for the bulge in his back pocket. It did seem odd, though, as Nicole had someone... Jim, was his name, on a regular basis. Early weekend mornings, Sinclair would see Jim departing the elevator, then the building. Jim cringed when their eyes met.

For whatever their reasons, it wasn't Sinclair's business, but it made conversation at his breakfast table.

"Hello, anyone here?" Sinclair shouted while standing in Neve's entryway. No one answered. Nothing seemed too out-of-place as he went farther in. Of course, he didn't know for sure, as he'd only been in the apartment two or three times. Neve occasionally locked herself out. He was about to step into the living room when he noticed his wife standing by Neve's front door...phone in hand.

"Check her bedroom," she said as she turned on a lamp in the living room.

Sinclair's hands grew cold. He didn't like any of this. He thought about protesting, all the while obeying his wife's command. On the floor outside the threshold was a shirt and other clothing. He glanced through the open doorway.

"Oh, my God." Neve was lying on her bed face down, nude except for a thong, her arm dangling. "Neve, are you all right?"

She didn't respond.

He glanced over his shoulder. "Call for an ambulance."

It didn't take long for the emergency services to arrive. This was the Gold Coast, after all, and Sunday night, which usually wasn't busy. Sinclair didn't have answers to many of their questions, but he did manage to give one of the EMTs Neve's purse.

* * *

Hours later, Sinclair looked at the clock near his bed. It was past midnight, early Monday morning, and sleep had not come. Tossing and turning, he'd close his eyes and visualized Neve's naked body. Not that he would or could do anything about it. Always the what if… and then reality butted in. The image faded, replaced by the discussion he and his wife had regarding Neve. What happened to her? Their chat reached no conclusion.

Sinclair lay awake, still disturbed. Neve. He looked over at his wife, sound asleep as usual. She could sleep through a hurricane.

Unlike Nicole, who rarely spoke to him, Neve was friendly. He had a fairly good idea Neve was, in his view, a free spirit. He didn't judge as he too had lived as if tomorrow didn't matter. He quietly got out of bed and reached for his bathrobe, then tiptoed to his entryway. He heard the muffled ring of the elevator's call button. Strange. *Who the…is it Neve?* He opened his front door and listened. The elevator's motor whined, then he heard the sound of rushing footsteps. *What the hell was going on?* He grabbed the baseball bat he kept in the front closet. He climbed the stairs passing the elevator car as it went to the lobby. Neve's door appeared secured. He looked up to the third floor.

A door gently closed.

Chapter Fifty-Four

Jim stared at Whirley. "What the fuck are you doing? Leave me alone."

"I'm not letting you off so easy. You helped kill a cop."

She was stronger than he thought as he twisted his body and grabbed her forearm. "I don't know what's in your head, but I did nothing. Annie turned out to be crazy. I had nothing to do with what she did, or Nicole."

"R-i-g-h-t— Who? Nicole?"Whirley gritted her teeth. "That's why you ran off before the cops arrived. The man lying on that ground was a friend."

"A what? You knew that guy. Holy shit. You do get around."

He felt her grip loosening. Her face contorted and a tear slid down the side of her cheek.

"Sorry about…about that friend. But it doesn't excuse what you did to me the other night. You knew all the time that asshole was in the apartment ready to snap those photos to use as blackmail. You're the cause of all of this." He pried her hand from his shoulder, then held onto her.

"Let go, or you'll be in even more shit than you are."

"Yeah? I'm in control now. There's no boogie man to save you. Who sent you to spy on me at that restaurant? Was it Hill? That cop?"

"Let go of me, you bastard."

Jim grabbed her around the waist and dragged her into the alley, then shoved her. "Answer the question." She fell against a dumpster. He stood over her, his chest heaving, then realized messing with her would only add to his woes. "Sorry," he said it haltingly. "You've got to…"

She rubbed the back of her head, then her neck. "Stay away from me."

He took a small step back. "Sure, no problem. I'm not the one doing the chasing." He glanced towards the mouth of the alley. "Give me your phone." He stuck his arm out. "Come on…"

Whirley found her footing and stood up. "Are you out of your mind? I'm not giving you anything."

"I mean it." A light switched on from the rear of Neve's apartment momentarily distracting him. He guessed it came from the kitchen. Neve was home or…

Whirley made a quick move to escape. Jim dove and caught her leg. She fell and screamed. Car lights pierced the darken alley.

"Oh shit," Jim said, releasing her leg. Big mistake. Whirley kicked him in the side of his mouth. It stunned him, but the pain hadn't registered. He saw her struggle to her knees. He lurched for her again and landed on the gravel. He didn't hear the car door open. A pair of well-polished shoes stood in front of him, and they weren't Whirley's.

"Get up," the man dressed in a sport coat said.

Jim groaned from the pain.

"I'm not going to repeat myself. Do it now."

Jim slowly raised himself to his knees. Everything hurt. The man stood two to three feet away. Whirley sat on the ground with her phone in her hand.

"You won't need that," the man said. He stooped and grabbed Whirley's cell.

* * *

Hill parked his car. This time he got lucky. The space was in front of Neve's apartment. Things were looking up. He stuffed all the misfortune of the day to the back of his mind: Lori, Skinny, Jim, everything. He took a breath and looked up at the apartment. It was dark. The hussy thought that would fool him. She didn't know who she was dealing with. He'd take his triumph and when he was through, he'd give JK a report while in the bedroom fondling and doing whatever he liked to JK's daughter.

And Neve? Oh, Neve would be in a fetal position, whimpering from all her exertions. He'd have her listen to the call, unable and more importantly unwilling to contradict him. It would be a grand reward for a miserable day.

He had a smile plastered on his face as he grabbed the door handle. His phone beeped. "Damn it." He had half a mind not to answer, then he recognized the number.

"JK, I was going to call you."

"Uh-huh. Listen, Hill, my police sources told me about Skinny and the broad's—what's her name? Laura? Lisa? Lori… something's…. death. I don't like it. It's bad, Goddamn bad publicity. Have you or the cops found that character, Jim?"

"Not yet, working on it."

"Jim is the key, Hill. Clean up the mess."

"Yes sir, of course."

"And Hill, make sure my daughter gets home and stays there. You're still at the hospital, right?"

Hill looked around. "Yes sir, I am."

"Good. The nurse I spoke with said Neve should be released any minute."

Hill checked his watch and twisted his face. "That's the information I have."

"All right. Call me as soon as my damn daughter is bedded down for the night. And Hill, don't screw this up."

Hill heard dead air and stared at his phone. Should he change his plans? He sat in his car, door open, with one foot resting on the curb. He glanced at the building again. *The boss told me to bed her down,* he laughed. Hill gestured a mock salute. "Will do." He got out of the car and used his key to open the security door of Neve's building. Even though her apartment was only on the second floor, it had been a long day and longer night. He'd wait for the elevator and conserve his strength for more important things.

The elevator took its time as it usually did. Strangely, Hill didn't mind. He took his flashlight from his back pocket. The key to Neve's door was in his hands. The arrival of the car with its familiar shudder interrupted his thoughts. He slid the steel gate open, then let it shut behind him. He pushed the button on the panel for the second floor. The motor moaned and the elevator slowly ascended. He realized he left his gloves in the car right before it came to its stop. No matter, he was supposed to be there—looking after the little lamb. He chuckled and exited. He leisurely walked the few feet to Neve's door and stuck the key in the lock. He thought he heard something above him. He paused, looked up, then shrugged. Nicole was dead. No one could be up there. He opened Neve's door and stepped in. His flashlight was bright, but the beam was focused. He stepped as quietly as he could going from one room to the other. Her bedroom was how he had left it…but no Neve. He searched all the closets, searched the living room, dining room, pantry. He flicked on the kitchen light. She wasn't to be found. He retraced his steps, even looking under her bed. His anger built. He returned to the dining room. He scanned the room and noticed the chest of drawers in the corner. One, on the bottom, was not quite closed. He pulled it open and saw it was empty. He stared at the space; his palm rested on the handle. It wasn't a large drawer, but big enough to hold papers. A key perhaps. Nicole's? His anger dissipated. It all clicked. He gazed upwards. In a few minutes the scamp would be corralled. The irony of doing her in Nicole's bed was delicious.

He marched out of Neve's apartment and clambered up the stairs. He drew his gun. No more surprises.

Chapter Fifty-Five

Hill was near the third-floor landing when he saw a shadow by Nicole's door. He didn't ask any questions and fired his weapon. It hit the mark. The man fell, his bat rolled down the stairs toward Hill. He sidestepped the piece of lumber and ran up the two remaining steps. Neve must have opened the door. She stood in the doorway.

"The guy was about to break in," Hill said.

Her jaw trembled. "What did you do? He's my neighbor. You killed him!"

Hill moved quickly past the man and pushed Neve inside. "You got it wrong. He was about to attack you and I saved your ass."

He came at her, gun in hand. His presence a foot in front of her pressing her to retreat. Each step took them closer to Nicole's bedroom.

"Get out. You're a murderer. That's not what happened."

"Privileged bitch." He slapped her. "Was he also one of your lovers? Either way you're going to call the police and tell them the story I tell you. Not right away, though. You and I have unfinished business."

Her eyes bulged. "I…I…" She rubbed the spot where he'd struck her.

He tore at her sweatshirt. "Take it off. I want to see your titties." He heard himself say those words. How uncharacteristic of him, but he found it enjoyable not to be restrained either by himself or anyone else. Tonight, he would allow himself to be. "Go on. I don't have all night."

She crisscrossed her arms over her chest. "No, I won't."

"You little bitch. You think you'll defy me?"

He knocked her down, then straddled her.

* * *

Sinclair's senses returned to him slowly. He heard his breathing, then touched his arms and checked the rest of himself. The bastard came close but missed. He realized he was lying on the third-floor landing outside Nicole's. As he worked himself to a sitting position, he heard the commotion inside the apartment. Whatever was happening was bad. He crawled to the stairs and retrieved his bat. He knew he was crazy and if he survived, he'd have his wife to deal with, but he had to help. He glanced down the stairwell. There was no one else, and no more time. He got to his feet and entered Nicole's apartment. It didn't take much to figure out where they were. He went down the hallway to the living room and saw the man on top of Neve. Her arms flailed. The stranger was tearing at her clothes. Sinclair had been an amateur golfer and knew how to swing a club. He didn't miss. The stranger fell to the side.

"Mr. Watson." Neve heaved his name. He took a step toward her. He didn't see the gun. This time he felt the bullet and he fell, sounds and light drifting away.

* * *

The man in the alley demanded Jim and the woman get up. They were going into Neve's building. He made it clear that refusal was not an option.

"You're Jim," he told him, "I know all about you. And you, lady, are Whirley. Your friend, Joe, or you may know him as Skinny, died tonight in a car accident."

"Oh, my God," Whirley covered her face with her arms. "Joe? Dead?"

"There'll be time to cry. Let's go."

The man herded them into the building. "We'll take the stairs. The elevator is too slow, but you knew that, Jim, right?"

Jim didn't respond.

They reached the second floor. Neve's door was open. They heard noise and a thump from above.

"Move it," the man ordered.

They ran up the stairs and entered Nicole's apartment. When they reached the living room, Hill sat bleeding from the side of his head. A pool of blood gathered on the rug next to the prone body of another man. Neve, her sweatshirt ripped, her face bruised, was on the floor near Hill, shaking.

"Mr. Hill?"

Hill snapped to the direction of the voice. His mouth opened. He raised his hand and made garbled sounds.

"Mr. Hill, I'm talking to you."

Hill tried to rise but fell back. He stuttered and finally replied, "JK?"

Chapter Fifty-Six

Charlie violated the law by checking her text messages while driving. Reading Neve's, a shiver of fear, then frustration swept over her—Neve.

Charlie's vehicle veered into the next lane. Horns blare. *Holy shit.* By the grace of God, she avoided hitting the car. This was too much, too many losses and near ones. Charlie wiped her face. She was out of cigarettes. *Have to think, regain my composure.* Neve was alive, thank God, but now this… She slammed her fist on the center console.

She glanced out the window and realized by some miracle she'd got herself off the expressway and onto North Avenue. With any luck, she was ten minutes from Neve's apartment. No stopping for lights. She was a cop.

Charlie pulled up to Neve's building. A quick search for parking spaces left her with no choice. She double-parked and left her vehicle running, lights flashing. She ran out of her car into the building. She ignored the elevator and with her heart pumping, attacked the stairs, drawing her personal revolver. At the second floor landing she saw Neve's open door. She edged towards it. "Neve?" She listened and debated whether to enter. She glanced toward the stairwell that led to Nicole's and noticed a thin beam of light drizzling the stairs, then a thud and voices. Holy shit, Hill and Neve were upstairs.

She walked up the flight, working the shadows. On the landing, outside Nicole's door, she clearly heard someone speaking. She knew Nicole's layout well and had a good idea where that person was. She entered quietly and made herself as small a target as she could hugging the hallway wall.

Charlie burst into the living room; her arms outstretched in front of her pointing her weapon. "Freeze! Police!" She took in the room. The male with his hand on the side of his bleeding scalp sitting on the floor next to Neve must be Hill. She stooped and grabbed his gun. She didn't know the female near Jim. Jim? What the...? The body on the floor...oh my God that's the neighbor...Sinclair Watson. She ordered them not to move, then went over, knelt, and felt for a pulse, then whipped out her phone.

"What are you doing?" A male in a sports jacket stood on the other side of Neve, behind a high-back chair.

Young glared. "Nine-one-one. Who the fuck are you?"

"Hold on, now. We know each other."

Charlie stared. "You must..."

Neve spoke, "Daddy."

"Shut up, dear," JK said. He smiled and was about to take a step forward.

"Don't you dare." Young raised her gun and looked over to Neve. "What happened?"

"She doesn't know," JK intervened. He spoke slowly. "As I said, we know each other thanks to Nicole and her little book. Nicole wrote down everything. You're 'L.' Besides, you worked for me. I had you inform on my little slut, my daughter, what she was doing on my dime. Good job." He laughed. "You even went beyond and according to Nicole, you knew my daughter, shall we say, intimately." He turned to Neve. "Isn't that right?" He didn't wait for an answer. "You even got to know Jim, over there. Didn't you?"

Charlie got to her feet. "Where are you going with this?"

JK placed his hands under his chin, as if in prayer, then smiled. "Mr. Hill, what happened here?"

Hill looked up. He held one hand on his wound. "Well, sir, as you instructed, I...eh...was, I mean I brought Neve home from the hospital. She had overdosed. She didn't want to stay at her apartment and went upstairs."

"Liar."

"Be a good girl, Neve," JK said.

Hill continued, "I came up the stairs to check on Neve and that guy attacked me." He pointed to the man lying in a pool of blood. "I shot at him in the hallway. Neve opened the door. I told her to get into the apartment for her safety. We went down the hallway, and when we got into the living room, that man appeared out of nowhere and struck me with a bat. I fell. I didn't know who he was. When he went toward Neve, I shot him."

Neve had tears running down her face, shaking her head, "No. It's not true," she said hoarsely.

Her father stepped towards her and slapped the side of her face. "I told you to be quiet."

Charlie brought her gun forward. "Do that again and you'll regret—"

"What. What will I regret, Detective Young? Look around this room, you're standing in the same shit. One word from me or Mr. Hill and your career is gone."

"Is that a threat?"

JK smiled. "Absolutely not. It's just a fact. So, here we are, Detective Young, at a juncture. How do we resolve it? As in any good negotiation, we all get something."

Charlie didn't want to listen but couldn't stop. The voice in her head shouted, *Your career. Everything you worked for…gone…puff.* Not only that but she could be looking at jail for planting evidence…and oh my God… She glanced at Hill who sat like a trained puppy waiting for his master. Jim and the woman stared, as if they were watching a play, and Neve. Poor Neve sat on the floor, rocking from side to side, biting her lip, her eyes red from tears.

JK continued, ignoring everyone but Charlie. "You, Detective, keep your job. No one will ever know your involvement. This," he waved his hand over the prone body "…whatever this is, gets written off as self-defense. I'll deal with Mr. Hill but in the meantime, he will continue to… eh…. protect Neve." He half-turned to Hill.

"That is what you want, right?"

Hill's eyes met JK's, a sheepish grin snaked across his lips.

"See," JK pronounced. "As for Jim, you're a suspect in two deaths."

"What are you talking about?" He took a step toward JK, but Whirley put her arm out to stop him and mouthed, *no.*

"The police believe you killed Nicole and maybe that friend or live-in companion Laur... Lori. That's her name."

Jim put his hands to his face. "Lori...Lori's dead? I can't...how?"

"Good acting, Jim. You're looking at jail, expensive trials, and maybe the police can prove it."

"Lori, was she in an accident? Tell me, Goddamn it!"

JK waited until his outburst was done.

"You are a sonofabitch. I didn't... I had nothing to do with any of it." He rubbed his eyes.

JK put his index finger to his mouth to silence him. "Then again, no one here would testify or knows anything about it. Isn't that true, Detective?"

Charlie continued to stare and lowered her weapon.

"Whirley..." He stopped. "You will continue your work for the company. Mr. Hill will see that you are well compensated." He paused, letting his words sink in, then clapped his hands together. "Like I said, everyone gets something."

"What do you get?" Charlie asked.

"I get the satisfaction that this is all swept under the rug. No publicity, my good name isn't sullied."

Charlie's throat was parched. She shifted her gaze and glanced at Neve. *What happens to your daughter?* "What about her?" Charlie found the courage to ask.

JK sneered. The muscles in his face tightened. "You want her, Detective?"

"What? I mean..."

"Don't bother. Neve is an embarrassment but will be taken care of as she always has been. Mr. Hill will see to that, as will I."

Silence settled over the room. No one moved. No one responded. Charlie glanced at Neve, then Hill. She avoided JK and looked over her shoulder at Sinclair. He had a pulse when she checked. If she did nothing, he'd die. She'd be complicit in his murder…a killer like any other murderer. If she acted, her career was gone.

"Everyone move back, including you, JK" She raised her weapon. She had to think. Who was she? She always had a good sense of right and wrong. What happened to her?

Her debate was interrupted by the sound of a creaking floorboard. Charlie was too late to respond. A woman rushed into the room.

"Sinclair. What did you do to my Sinclair?"

* * *

Neve seized the moment. She amazed herself that she had strength enough to move quickly by Hill to the couch where she had her purse. She was in reach when Daddy grabbed her shoulder. She kicked him in the balls. He doubled over.

"Shut up," Neve shouted, "it's my turn." She turned to JK. "You piece of garbage. Money isn't going to buy you out of this. I'm an embarrassment? Your whole life is a house of cards. You buy things and people and think you're righteous. You think I don't know how you snuck up here to fuck Nicole? I know."

JK was still hunched. "She's raving. It's the drugs," he choked out.

Neve kicked him again. He hit the floor. Neve went around the couch and approached Mrs. Watson. "Take my phone, call nine-one-one." Neve glared at Charlie, who didn't move.

"I know Nicole was murdered, and I know who did it." Neve reached into her bag and withdrew the evidence package. "You recognize this?" She held the plastic envelope showing it to Charlie, then stooped a bit to make sure Daddy saw it too. "It's the snifter by Nicole's bed. I found it after the police left the night Nicole died."

She turned to Jim. "You left Nicole that night near daybreak. Right?"

He nodded, his face pale.

"She was alive?"

"Yes…yes she was."

"I saw you leave. You took the elevator."

Jim nodded vigorously. "Yeah, I did."

Neve turned toward her daddy. "I heard another thump. Minutes after Jim left. You must have stayed in Nicole's apartment and got your rocks off watching the two of them. No matter, Nicole thought highly of your skills."

JK had one hand by his groin, struggling to stand.

"Daddy, you left your cigar at Nicole's. You should know better. Jim doesn't smoke." She turned to Charlie. "When you send this to the lab, you'll not only find Daddy's prints but wine residue. Nicole loved wine. Champagne not so much."

Neve paused and looked at Mrs. Watson. "How is he?"

"He's still among us." She patted her husband's face. "Here's your phone. I pressed Emergency."

"Open the window," Neve ordered the woman near Jim. Seconds passed, maybe a minute, before Neve became aware of the faint sounds of sirens. "I'll make it quick. Daddy knew Nicole was on antidepressants. He was familiar as to how they work, given his wife and me. I'll bet Nicole mentioned it in her tell-all. Nicole knew too much about the company and wanted more. She was coming after Daddy. Her ambition made her a threat. Right, Daddy? That's how you and Mr. Hill dispose of people who get in your way."

She looked directly at Charlie. "Make sure they test for Nardil; use enough of it in wine and it's fatal." She gripped the evidence tightly in her hand. "Time to choose, Charlie."

Charlie exhaled slowly. She looked away from Neve's glare. She eyed JK, who minutes before considered himself the master, the king, now on all fours grunting and wheezing like a pig. His hit man, Hill, revealed himself as a sniveling "yes" man. She took the bag from Neve. "You're right. Can't lie to myself forever." She pointed her gun at JK. "Sit by Hill. You're both under arrest."

Chapter Fifty-Seven

The old adage of nothing good happens after 2 a.m. was truth Jim could attest to. The police, emergency equipment, and personnel stormed Nicole's apartment. Charlie and Neve laid it out for the cops. Hill and JK were taken into custody.

Sinclair, his wife, and Neve sped off in ambulances. God willing, Sinclair would survive. The EMTs seemed to think he had a good chance.

Charlie told the arresting officers she'd follow them to the station. Everyone left but the three of them. They walked through the apartment. Charlie seemed lost in thought as they wandered into Nicole's bedroom. Charlie sat on the bed. "How did all this happen?" she asked no one in particular.

Jim was about to respond, shook his head, and sat down near her. Whirley stood in the doorway, her eyes wide, looking at the expensive furniture.

"A lot of good times happened in here," Jim said. "Guess we all got carried away. We didn't think or care of the cost…Lori." He rubbed his eyes. "I know sorry is too late. She didn't deserve it." He glanced at Charlie. He wasn't sure if she heard. "Anyway, it's in the past." He slapped his leg. "Got to move on."

Whirley stepped into the room. "Well, Nicole did all right while she had it. Think of it this way, most of us don't have the courage or will to live out fantasies. We're screwed by our own reality."

Charlie raised her head and sighed. "Let's go."

Charlie locked Nicole's door and put the key in her pocket. She turned to Jim and Whirley. "The price was too high…way too high."

They chose the elevator for old times' sake. It was a relic and there probably wouldn't be another opportunity. The ride was of course slow, but no one was in a hurry. Once outside Charlie said, "Good-bye" and went to her double-parked car. She leaned over the driver's side and grabbed something from the windshield. She waved it as if it was diseased.

"Can you believe it? After all this…a goddamn parking ticket!" She got in her car, slammed her door, and drove off.

Jim squinted, wetted his lips, and watched her rumble down the street. "Charlie, Charlie," he said more to himself. His sigh was wistful. "She did the right thing. Whatever happens, she'll land on her feet."

"I know that look, Jim." Whirley interrupted. "Charlie does have a great bod. Did you miss out?"

Jim raised his eyebrows and smiled. "Coffee?"

She shrugged, "Why not. I'm famished, too."

"All right, then.

They were two of a kind. Sort of made for each other.